Her breath tightened in her chest.

She couldn't believe her ears. Max had given her up to the authorities. Was this why he'd brought her here? To set her up?

"Daisy, I can explain."

She pushed past him and ran outside, but Max stepped out behind her. "I called my brother because he's an undercover detective. I want to protect you, Daisy."

"I never asked you to protect me!"

"Fine." He stepped back. "If you want to keep running, then go. But the baby stays with me. I won't let anybody hurt him."

"I don't want to run anymore." She grabbed his hand in both of hers. "I just want this nightmare to be over."

"Then trust me."

The irony wasn't lost on her. She'd never trusted anyone, and he didn't rescue people. Yet here they were.

Before she could respond, headlights swamped the porch and a voice barked, "On your knees, both of you! This time you talk...or you die."

Maggie K. Black is an award-winning journalist and romantic suspense author with an insatiable love of traveling the world. She has lived in the American South, Europe and the Middle East. She now makes her home in Canada with her history-teacher husband, their two beautiful girls and a small but mighty dog. Maggie enjoys connecting with her readers at maggiekblack.com.

Books by Maggie K. Black

Love Inspired Suspense

True North Heroes

Undercover Holiday Fiancée
The Littlest Target

True North Bodyguards

Kidnapped at Christmas
Rescue at Cedar Lake
Protective Measures

Killer Assignment
Deadline
Silent Hunter
Headline: Murder
Christmas Blackout
Tactical Rescue

Visit the Author Profile page at Harlequin.com.

THE LITTLEST TARGET

MAGGIE K. BLACK

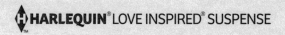

Recycling programs
for this product may
not exist in your area.

LOVE INSPIRED BOOKS

ISBN-13: 978-1-335-54364-6

The Littlest Target

Copyright © 2018 by Mags Storey

www.Harlequin.com

Printed in U.S.A.

For thou hast been a strength to the poor,
a strength to the needy in his distress, a refuge
from the storm, a shadow from the heat, when the
blast of the terrible ones is as a storm against the wall.
—Isaiah 25:4

Thanks as always to my agent Melissa Jeglinski,
my editor Emily Rodmell and the rest of the
Love Inspired team who encourage authors like me
and bring stories like these to life.

ONE

Daisy Hayward brushed a kiss over nine-month-old Fitz Pearce's tender head and gently lowered him into the crib, just as a deafening crash sounded through the darkened country house below. The baby's eyes shot open. Fitz's lip quivered. Tears filled his anxious gaze. Instantly, Daisy plucked her tiny charge from the crib and held him to her chest to rock him back to sleep. He nestled against her. The pervasive anxiety that seemed to fill little Fitz's unhappy home tightened around her heart like a vise.

Lord, I feel so trapped in this miserable place. Sometimes, I don't know how much I can take.

In the eight and a half months since she'd become Fitz's nanny, there'd been moments when she'd almost felt like a prisoner in the remote Quebec countryside estate. Endless days of long, uncomfortable tension stretched whenever Gerald Pearce was away on business, only to then erupt into angry shouts and paranoid accusations between him and his young second wife, Anna, whenever he came home.

For Daisy, growing up in a small English village where jobs were scarce, being hired to care for the son of a wealthy Canadian computer developer had felt like a dream come true. It wasn't until she'd arrived in Canada that she'd discovered the truth. Fitz's mother, Jane Pearce, had died in childbirth. A hasty wedding to Anna, one of Pearce Enterprises's lead graphic designers and almost thirty years Gerald's junior, had followed. But despite being newlyweds, their relationship was fraught with shouted accusations and slamming doors, and even one late night visit from two police officers. None of which was helped by Daisy's suspicions that Gerald's paranoid and scattered mind was slipping.

She could hear things breaking now, as if Anna and Gerald had given up on shouting and decided instead to trash their expensive home. Fitz's pudgy hand grabbed a fistful of her long blond hair and held it tightly. She slid a finger between his gums and felt the telltale bump of a new tooth getting ready to come through. He was teething.

Daisy tightened her arms around him.

"Don't worry," she whispered. "I've got you. You're safe. I'm not going anywhere."

There was nowhere to go and reminding herself of that always helped somehow. The estate was in the middle of nowhere, and they didn't need gates or fences to keep her there. In fact, Anna often told her with her smug little smile that she was free to leave on her days off and then wouldn't let her use the car.

Daisy gritted her teeth and refused to let her eyes even consider forming tears. It wasn't like there was anything good waiting for her back home either. Her stepfather was a drunk and a thief, her mother hadn't put up much of a fight when Daisy had been first kicked out of the house seven years ago—when she was just sixteen—and now there were four tiny half siblings back home that her mother desperately needed Daisy's pay to help feed.

Lord, if reminding myself of that is what keeps me here, then please don't ever let me forget. Fitz needs me. I can't imagine what would happen to him without me.

Anna screamed and her shrill voice rose above the noise, so clearly it was as if she was standing on the other side of the door. "No! Don't shoot! Please!"

Then, before she could even blink, a sudden deafening crack seemed to split the air. Anna's screams died. Fitz howled.

Daisy's heart smacked inside her slender frame, telling her to move, even as her brain scrambled to think. She crossed the nursery, slid the door open and positioned herself in the doorway so that she could look out, while keeping the child in her arms still sheltered behind her. She glanced over the landing.

Two of Gerry's business associates were tossing the place. Silent and hulking, with bald heads and cold stares, she'd always imagined that "Mr. Smith" and "Mr. Jones" had been carved from the same block of cement. She'd always wondered if those were their real names and found them almost indistinguishable except for the fact that Smith's large nose was crooked and Jones had an ugly scar on his throat. Considering Gerry's creeping paranoia, Daisy had always guessed they were some form of security. Now Smith was knocking over shelves and tossing glass and ceramics to the floor, while Jones took a knife to the furniture.

Then she saw Anna, lying still on the floor of the grand foyer, her long fair hair and dress stained from the dark pool of blood spreading out from what looked like a gunshot wound deep in her chest. For a moment, panic curled like smoke inside Daisy's throat, choking out her ability to think or even move.

Then Smith grunted and said, "I'll finish down here. You go do the baby's room."

Jones turned toward the stairs, knife in hand. Daisy ducked back into the nursery, closed the door and locked it. Then shifting Fitz to her hip, she wedged a chair under the door. She doubted it would hold long. Her eyes scanned the nursery, piled high with stuffed animals, model trucks, electronic gizmos and plastic toys, all meant for a child much older than Fitz. Gerry seemed to think that every weekend he came home required giving his son a gift.

She slid on the chest carrier and buckled Fitz in, then zipped her raincoat over them both, so that his head poked out the top. His cries faded to whimpers. She dashed into the walk-in closet that served as her room, grabbed the rucksack she'd brought from England and tossed in a change of clothes for herself, more clothes for Fitz, his blanket, diapers and bottles.

Unfortunately, her cracked cell phone hadn't worked in days; not since it had died at the hands of Fitz's obsession with pushing buttons and grabbing anything shiny and electronic he could get his hands on.

Footsteps sounded on the landing. Jones was on his way. Daisy yanked the nursery window open, swung her leg over the ledge, reached for the trellis and climbed down, praying with each step that it would hold their weight. She heard the crash of the nursery door burst open, then the sound of Jones cursing.

She hit the ground. Her feet pounded around the side of the house. A pair of headlights raced toward her. Her hands rose to block the glare. Then she heard an engine stop and Gerry's befuddled voice. "Daisy? What are you doing out here?"

She stumbled toward the sound. "We need to call 911. Anna's been shot."

"What? Who?" He grabbed her arm.

She prayed his reaction was from shock. His memory gaps had been getting more frequent, even though she'd always assumed a man in his fifties was too young for dementia.

"Your new wife, Anna." She blinked and her vision cleared. His gray hair and beard were an odd, sickly yellow in the glare of his sports car headlights. "Anna was shot, in your house, just now. Smith and Jones shot her. We need to call an ambulance and the police."

"No, not Smith and Jones. They wouldn't hurt Anna. They're loyal to me." His hand tightened its grip until she could almost feel bruises forming, then he dropped her arm as suddenly as he'd grabbed it. "I will call the police. I know which ones I can trust. But you— you have to stay away from the police, okay? There are some corrupt cops who are out to steal my work and they will hurt Fitz to do it. Two of them came to the house. They threatened me and tried to blackmail me. You have to promise me you won't let them hurt Fitz."

"Of course." Panic crawled up her throat. She remembered those cops. There'd been two of them, one man and one woman. But could she really believe any of his ranting? "I promise, I won't let anyone hurt Fitz."

"Good." Gerry blinked and she saw clarity return to his eyes. "Everything is going to be all right. I have an apartment in Sault Sainte Marie. Take Fitz there. Don't stop. Don't talk to anyone. I'll call a cop I know I can trust and get them to meet you there. I have very powerful enemies who are trying to steal my work and they will use Fitz to do that. But you and Fitz will be safe at my apartment, and I'll meet you there as soon as I can."

He reached into the sports car and programmed an address into the GPS. There was a car seat buckled into the back seat and next to it a large wooden sailboat with a bright red bow.

Gerry pushed a cell phone into her hand. "Text me when you get there. I'll take care of Anna. If I can find a police contact who I know isn't corrupted, I'll text you and send you to them. I can't promise this line is secure, though, so be careful who you call. Trust me, Daisy, do what I say and everything will be okay."

She didn't trust him. Not fully. But Gerry was her boss. If she refused, then what? It wasn't like running back into the house was an option.

Fitz whimpered. Gerry reached out, brushed a gentle touch over his head and leaned in toward his son. "You're the best thing I ever made. We'll play with your toys again soon."

A shout came from behind them. Jones was running toward them, weapon drawn. Gerry yanked a gun from his belt.

"Daisy!" he shouted. "Go! I'll hold him off!"

She yanked the back door open and buckled Fitz inside, then she climbed into the driver's seat and turned the key. The car purred beneath her. She glanced at the GPS. It told her she was facing a ten-and-a-half-hour drive to Sault Sainte Marie across northern Ontario.

A hail of bullets sounded in the darkness. She put the car in Reverse and glanced in the rearview mirror. Her eyes fell on Fitz's startled face through his tiny car seat mirror. One hand clutched the yellow sail of his new toy boat. "Don't worry, Fitz. I'll keep you safe. I promise."

Just as soon as she figured out how to do that.

Lord, I don't know where this place is that I'm going or what it is I'm doing. I wish for once, there was someone, somewhere, I could count on not to throw my entire life into chaos. All I know right now is that I need to run.

More bullets sounded, mixed with shattering glass. She gunned the car backward, spun on the driveway and drove off into darkness. She followed the tiny blue line on the GPS, as the Pearce country estate exploded in a ball of fire and flames behind her.

"At least one body has been recovered from the remains of an apparent gas explosion around six thirty last night at the home of computer developer Gerald Pearce, outside Montreal. Fire crews remain on the scene hours after the explosion, battling to keep flames from spreading to the surrounding trees. Despite the rain being forecast, skies remain clear as a column of smoke and flame—"

Max Henry leaned across the cab of the rapid-response emergency vehicle and switched the radio off. His eyes darted to the clock. Was it after midnight already?

It had been three hours since he'd left University of Ottawa, where he'd given a talk to students on why they should consider careers as rural community and wilderness paramedics. He'd stuck around for an extra couple of hours to listen in on a talk from the air-ambulance pilots. They'd teased him about the fact that although he'd learned to fly, he'd never got around to getting his license, which meant he was always stuck in the back of the helicopters.

Now the night fell deep and heavy around him as he drove through the narrow, winding rural roads that would lead him through the Ontario woodlands back home to Huntsville.

The story about the Pearce mansion fire had been at the top of the news ever since he'd got in the vehicle. He'd heard of the Pearces of course. Probably most people had. Not that he knew much about them beyond seeing the pictures of their small but lavish wedding splashed all over news a few months back. Newly wealthy, reportedly brilliant and quite conventionally attractive, Anna Pearce had made quite a few glossy magazine covers since then. But Max didn't care about the gossip. Instead, every time the news story played, he couldn't help but map the emergency-response scenario out in his mind. A rapid-response unit like his would've got there first, he guessed. Followed almost immediately by police, who would secure the scene. Then ambulances and fire trucks and eventually news crews.

Silence filled the truck, punctuated only by the drone of the engine beneath him. He tapped his fingers on the steering wheel and tried to figure out how long it would be until a good radio music station would be in range. The temptation to turn the emergency scanners on niggled at him like an itch he couldn't reach between his shoulder blades.

He ran his hand over the back of his neck, feeling the telltale curl that told him that his dark shaggy hair was overdue for another haircut. He chuckled. He might technically be off shift, but when he left the conference, he hadn't even bothered to change out of his uniform into civvies.

There's supposed to be more to life than

work, Max. A voice floated in the back of his mind. It sounded suspiciously like his dad's new favorite topic. *You don't want to look up from work one day and realize you haven't actually lived.*

But why not? He argued back against the voice. And what qualified as living? Time off? A family? A white picket fence? A beautiful wife? A life spent speeding to accident scenes and leaping out of helicopters to save countless lives was hardly a waste.

Besides, it was all Trent's fault for putting these thoughts in their folks' heads. For as long as he could remember, the four Henry brothers had an unspoken pact to remain bachelors for life. Jacob, Nick and Max had all stuck to the deal.

Then his detective brother had the audacity to bring fellow detective Chloe home at Christmas. The next thing they knew, the couple's engagement cover story was the real deal—sweet romance and all.

Something rumbled behind him. His green eyes narrowed as he looked in the rearview mirror. The sports car behind him was gaining on him too quickly.

His lips set in a grim line and for a moment, he felt tempted to switch on his emergency lights just to slow them down. There was nothing worse than a reckless driver. Usually just the sight of an emergency vehicle on the road would be enough to make even the worst driver reduce speed. But either the sports car driver hadn't seen him or was in too big of a hurry to care. He nudged his truck over to the side of the road.

The sports car passed. Max turned and his eyes met the driver's for barely an instant. Then she sped away and was gone, leaving the afterimage of the brief glimpse he'd got of her in the glow of the dashboard lights seared on his mind.

It had been a woman. She'd been in her early twenties, he guessed, with long blond hair, huge eyes, a slender frame and a tight grip on the steering wheel. Questions as to what her story was filled his mind as he watched her taillights speed away ahead of him. She had looked terrified and determined, and there'd been something captivating about her that he couldn't put into words.

Then the telltale flicker of blue and white lights flashed in his rearview mirror. A sedan sped up behind him now—dark, plain and unmarked except for the LED flights flashing through the windshield. Well, whoever she was, she wouldn't get far with that unmarked police car on her tail.

He slowed his rapid-response vehicle to let the police car pass. It didn't even signal. Instead, it whipped around so close it would've clipped him if Max hadn't swerved.

A prayer for God's mercy thudded in Max's rib cage. A police officer should know better than to drive like that. Yet he watched, helpless and almost incredulous, as the unmarked car sped toward the blonde in the sports car. It nudged closer and closer to her, until it was tailgating dangerously. Cop or not, anyone driving that dangerously at speeds like that was flirting with disaster.

Then it happened, with a crunch of metal and a screech of tires. The unmarked police vehicle clipped the sports car. Max's heart lurched as he watched the blonde's vehicle spin. She was going to crash, right there in front of him, and all he could do was pray and try to steer his way clear.

He yanked the wheel hard to the right, pressing down on the brake as much as he dared without risking locking the brakes. Gravel sprayed beneath his tires. Trees spun past the windshield. From somewhere beyond him, he heard an agonizing screech of metal reverberating through the morning air. The sports car had smashed into something.

God, keep me from crashing into her!

The rapid-response truck slammed to a stop and he felt the back corner hit a rock with the kind of crunch that had him guessing he'd be looking at a new bumper and a little bit of bodywork when he got back home.

He looked up through the windshield. The sports car wasn't as well-off. The front end was embedded in a thick pine tree and the airbag had deployed. He just hoped the driver was all right.

No signal on his cell phone. He grabbed his CB radio and clipped it to his shoulder, ready to call in backup the second he assessed the scene and coordinated with the lead officer. As first on the scene, it was the cop's job to make the call.

Max grabbed the bright red jump bag that held all his basic medical necessities, slung it over his shoulder and ran toward the accident. The police car had stopped. In the dim headlights, he watched as a large man with a bald head ran toward the sports car, reached it first and yanked the driver's door open.

"My name is Max Henry, and I'm an Ontario paramedic!" Max shouted. "Stay back and let me assess injuries!"

The man didn't even turn. Instead he reached into the car, grabbed the driver and pulled her out. She screamed. The man threw her to the ground and forced her down onto her knees. A baby's wail filled the air. Max's heart stopped. There was an infant in the car!

"Get back in your truck and let me handle this!" the bald man thundered at him. "This woman is a dangerous criminal and I'm taking her into custody for murder and kidnapping!"

"He's lying!" the blonde yelled. Her accent was British, the kind that made him think of royalty and the Tower of London. She was kneeling down on the ground with one palm pressed into the pavement. Strength battled the vulnerability in her face. But it was the defiance in her eyes that made his breath catch.

The wail of the baby grew louder. Max listened carefully. It was the strong and hearty yell of an infant who was several months old, and definitely a howl of anger, rather than a whimper of pain or distress. Thankfully.

Max raised his hands and took a step forward. "Please, Officer, I'm not trying to get in your way, just let me make sure the baby and driver are both okay."

"Max, listen to me!" The sound of his name on the young woman's lips seemed to shake something inside his chest. "I'm not kidnapping this baby, and I didn't kill anyone. I promise. I'm his nanny. This man's name is Smith. He's not a cop. He's a killer. He murdered the baby's stepmother—"

Her words were swallowed up in a cry as Smith cuffed her hard on the back of her head. Max's jaw set. This stopped here and now.

"Step away from her with your hands up!" Max shouted. "If you really are a cop, I demand you show me your badge, although I'm pretty sure that despite the pretty flashing police lights on the car, which I now presume you've stolen, you don't have one." He grabbed the CB radio from his shoulder. "I'm calling this in."

Smith reached around his back. A Glock flashed in his hands so quickly Max barely had time to process what had happened. But there it was, with its barrel focused on Max's face.

"Drop the radio and get down on the ground now," Smith ordered. "Hands behind your head. Or I will shoot you where you stand."

TWO

Max froze. *Okay, Lord, now what do I do?* He'd faced more than his fair share of criminals without the benefit of a weapon or bulletproof vest. In fact, he'd just finished telling an auditorium full of fresh-faced university students that paramedics were attacked and injured more often than those in any other lifesaving career, and that he'd personally taken more blows to the jaw, punches, kicks and attempted stabbings than he liked to remember. But a bullet? This would be a first.

"I said, let her go." Max's voice rose. Gun or not, there was no way he was backing down now. "I will not let you hurt them."

Even if it meant fighting to his dying breath. The nanny's right hand darted behind her back. Smith aimed the gun at Max's head. Something cold glinted in his eyes and suddenly

Max knew with crystal clear certainty this man would kill him without a moment's hesitation.

Oh, Lord, I really need Your help right now!

The nanny yanked a pair of scissors out from behind her back and plunged them into Smith's leg. He swore. The gun fired, its bullet flew high into the sky.

Max dived into a front roll, feeling the heavy fabric of his uniform take the impact as his body hit the pavement. The woman slipped from Smith's grasp and ran for the car.

Max charged, throwing himself at Smith and locking his own hands around the weapon before Smith could get off another shot. They wrestled for the gun, rolling on the ground, as Max battled to hold his own against a man twice his size. He heard the sound of a car seat carrier unclicking from its base, a car door slamming and footsteps in the trees. The baby's cries faded into the distance.

The good news was it sounded like she'd got the baby safely out of the car. Bad news was it sounded like she was running.

The gun flew from Smith's grasp. Max sprang to his feet, only for Smith to level a sucker punch to his jaw that filled his eyes with stars. Smith darted for his vehicle. Max stood frozen for a second, uncertain which direction to run. But even before he heard the unmarked police car's door slam, he knew his answer. It wasn't his job to stop criminals. It was his job to save the lives of anyone who needed him.

Max took off running through the woods, following the sound of the nanny's footsteps and the baby's angry wail. He blinked as his eyes adjusted to the night around him. A woman and a baby alone in the woods, what did she think she was doing? Where did she think she was going?

Ahead of him he could hear her crashing through the trees. Behind him, the police car's engine roared and then faded back along the highway. Smith was leaving.

"Hey! Wait! It's okay!" Max called. "He's gone! You're safe!"

Then he could see her, dim in the moonlight, as she darted through the trees ahead of him with a bag on her shoulder and the baby in the car seat carrier clutched to her chest. He was gaining on her and so close that in another minute or two, he'd be able to touch her shoulder. She stopped, set the baby carrier down at her feet, spun back and raised the scissors.

"Stop! Right there!" she said. "Not another step! Or I'll stab you! I'm not kidding. I will not let you hurt Fitz."

"Oh, I totally believe you would stab me." Max froze. "And while I have more than enough gauze and bandages in my jump bag to patch myself up again, I really don't want to."

The corner of her lips twitched. His hands rose higher as his eyes ran over the baby. To his relief, the child looked fine and more surprised than hurt or scared. Still, a visual examination wasn't as accurate as a physical one would be.

"I promise, I only want to help, and Smith is gone," he said. "However he got his hands on an undercover cop car, I really don't believe he was an actual cop. You have nothing to fear now. It's just us three."

Cold March wind flickered between the trees. The baby whimpered softly. The woman reached down, tucked him deeper into the blankets and pulled the hood up over him. Where did she think she was going? The closest town was over an hour's drive away. She had no wheels, no shelter, nothing.

Nothing but him.

"I'm just reaching for my flashlight, okay?" he said. "It's on my belt. I just think this might go a bit easier if we can see each other better. All right?"

She nodded. He reached with one hand, clipped the light from his belt, switched it on and set it on the ground. A warm, yellow glow spread through the trees, casting the under-brush and branches in a maze of shifting shadows.

They both stepped forward into the light and his eyes scanned her slender frame. Her hair tumbled loose and wild around her shoulders. Her eyes were large, dark and luminous. Once again, the thought of British moors and royalty crossed his mind. It was like something out of one of those books his mother read, about beautiful and plucky countesses who escaped their captors, slipped from their prisons and ran with the royal heir.

Only, he was no fairytale hero. And whatever danger this woman was in that had her tearing through the woods and clutching a pair of scissors out in front of her like a weapon was all too real.

"I'm really not a criminal," she said again. "I didn't steal this baby and I didn't kill anyone."

"I hear you," Max said. He even had a hunch she was telling the truth. But that didn't mean he was about to let his guard down. He gestured to the badge on his shoulder. "I'm not a cop. Like I told you, I'm just a paramedic and I don't have the power to arrest anyone. It's my job to help people—even if they are criminals.

I'm just like a doctor, only with a lot more time spent working in the rain and getting covered by mud."

"Forgive me, but the fact you're in a uniform and waving a badge around doesn't immediately mean I'll trust you," she said. "I've met too many people like you who couldn't figure out the real truth of a situation if someone had smacked them on the head with it."

Something in the quiver of her chin told him there was a story there, and it wasn't a good one. "I'm sorry to hear that. I'll do my best to pay close attention to anything you hit me with."

Was it his imagination or had that very slight smile curled a little more at the corner of her lips?

"Thanks," she said. "I appreciate what you did back there. I really do. You probably saved our lives. But I don't want your help and I don't want you getting involved. Just tell me how to get to the next town and rent a car, and I'll take it from there."

He nodded slowly. "Why?" he asked.

"What do you mean why?" Her arms crossed and the scissors dropped to the ends of her fingertips. Okay, now they were getting somewhere. "I need a car, because the one I was driving is now wrapped around a tree."

"I mean, why won't you let me help you?" he asked. "It will take you hours to walk to the next town. It's supposed to rain eventually, even though the weather guys seem a bit late on that one. You're going to have a hard time finding anyone who'll rent you a car for at least nine hours. And something tells me you're not about to just hitchhike with some stranger."

"You're a stranger," she said.

Max felt a grin spreading across his face. He had to admit, weird as this was, he almost liked her. Sure, she was aggravating, stubborn and still might stab him. But there was something impressive about her, too. She had gumption as his dad would call it.

"Good point," he said. "Then let's get acquainted. As I shouted earlier while running toward a gunman, my name is Max Henry. I'm a paramedic from Huntsville, Ontario. I have three brothers—two older and one younger— and no pets. Now, would you like me to toss you my wallet so you can check my ID?"

She smiled. "No, that's okay. My name is Daisy. This is Fitz. Like I said before, I'm his nanny."

He waited to see if she was going to tell him

anything more. The wind picked up, sending trees dancing with a sound like brushes on a steel drum. She pressed her lips together and stared him down. Guess that was all the info he was getting for now.

"It's nice to meet you, Daisy," Max said. "Who's Smith?"

Her slim shoulders rose and fell. "I don't know his full name. He worked for Fitz's dad until I'm guessing he double-crossed him. Fitz's dad warned me not to let him or anyone else near the baby and to take Fitz to Sault Sainte Marie."

Max whistled. "That's a long drive. You said he killed Fitz's mother?"

"Stepmother actually, but yeah," she said. "His mother died in childbirth."

Max felt an eyebrow rise. Dying in childbirth did happen, true, but it was very rare in Canada. Not to mention Fitz was less than a year old. Had Fitz's parents split up when she was pregnant? How quickly had Fitz's father remarried?

And was he going to learn any of these people's real full names?

He'd never met anyone so determined to tell him as little information as humanly possible, like she was slipping tiny scraps of it to him through the bars of a prison window.

"We need to call this in and let police know that a woman is dead," Max said as gently as he could.

"They know," she said. "It was on the news and I saw a police car fly past me as I was leaving."

Really, he couldn't remember hearing about any murders on the radio and a murder tended to be at the top of the news. There'd been a major fire reported in Quebec. But nothing that had involved a baby or a murdered woman. He clenched his jaw and fought the urge to dig.

WIN. The acronym he'd heard and used himself hundreds of times filled his mind. What's Important Now.

As fascinating as whatever murder mystery she was caught up in might be, it wasn't the most important thing right now. The most important thing was convincing her to get in his vehicle and let him take them to safety. Prying was tempting. But prying would also probably spook her and the last thing he needed was for her to run.

His arms crossed. Time to negotiate.

"Well, Daisy. You want to get to the nearest town and to get a vehicle. I want to double-check that Fitz is okay and give you a ride—"

"I also don't want the police involved." She cut him off. "Not until I'm convinced that I can trust them. Right now, all I know is that some cops want to hurt Fitz, and I don't know which cops I can trust."

He ran his hand through his dark shaggy hair. "Would you talk to a trustworthy and honest cop?"

"Yes, but when and how I do is a decision I get to make."

She was impossible. He had three cops in his family—Trent and his fiancée, Chloe, and his eldest brother, Jacob. Plus, his youngest brother, Nick, was in the military, which meant all four Henry brothers were in some form of uniformed lifesaving work. He pressed his lips together, debated telling her that and decided against it for fear it would spook her even worse.

"Well, I have to call the accident in," Max said. "What if someone else comes along and hits it? You think your boss wants you to leave his very expensive sports car wrecked at the side of the road?"

"You think he wants me to risk his baby's life for the sake of reporting a crashed car?"

Her voice matched the volume of his. "He's got plenty of cars. He's only got one son!"

Okay, maybe she had a point with that one. But Max was also pretty sure that her boss was a crook, which made her an accomplice to who knew what kind of crime. He ran his hand over the back of his neck. The frustration that burned there was less at her and more at Fitz's father and Smith and whatever dishonest and crooked things they were involved in that had cost Fitz's stepmother her life and had left Daisy out here alone, in the woods with a baby to protect.

The wind grew sharper. Fitz's whimpers turned to cries. Daisy leaned down and rocked him gently. Max could tell the baby was about to howl and was positive Daisy could tell that, too.

He ran his hand over his jaw and asked God to help him choose his words carefully.

"Look, you're obviously in trouble," he said, "and I obviously want to help. I've got a vehicle. It's plenty warm and comfortable. If you let me give you a ride to the next town, I promise I won't call 911, try to take you to a police station or pry anymore into your life. My responsibility is to make sure you're both okay, no matter your story. Now, please, will you let me do my job and help you?"

Silent prayers filled Daisy's heart, even as she could feel it beating like a drum. He had no idea how tempting his offer was, how long the last hours of driving had dragged on her limbs and just how much she wanted to be somewhere safe, away from the cold and the fear.

But she couldn't let her guard down. Smith had somehow found her and the fact that he'd also somehow got his hand on a police vehicle didn't do much to sway her concerns about Gerry's warning not to trust the cops. Plus, when she'd grabbed her bag and Fitz's car seat out of the wrecked remains of Gerry's smashed car, she'd found a brand-new prepaid burner cell phone and two envelopes of hundred-dollar bills that she guessed totaled at least a few grand on the floor of the back seat. She'd grabbed the phone on impulse in case anything happened to the one Gerry had given her and had stuffed the cash in her rucksack, figuring she'd need some money to take care of Fitz. It had been a split-second decision she'd made without thinking. Now, that the world was quiet again she wondered if it'd been the right one.

Could a burner phone be traced like a regular cell phone could? The phone looked like it had never even been activated. Would using it be more or less safe than using the phone Gerry had given her? She had no idea.

Max was still staring at her, waiting for her to say something. Her eyes roamed over him as if searching for answers to questions she couldn't even think to ask.

He was tall with broad shoulders and arms that hinted he was able to carry a lot more weight than his slender build implied. His dark hair was soaked with sweat, slightly messy and curling just a little at his neck. His blue paramedic uniform radiated reassurance and authority.

But then again, so had all the uniforms of the men who'd stood in her living room and listened to her stepfather's lies, while he denied he'd ever lost his temper and hit anyone, pressured her mom to say she was clumsy and branded Daisy hysterical.

Daisy's eyes met Max's again. They were green, with a look in their depths that spoke of protection, security and warmth. Suddenly she realized she was holding the scissors so loosely he could've probably knocked them from her fingers and taken it at any time. Her grip tightened. "I wasn't kidding when I said I will not let you hurt Fitz."

"Understood," he said. "I just want to take a look at him to make sure he's okay. He looks fine from here but I won't know for sure until I can take a more thorough look. Let's start by walking back to my vehicle where the light is better. Then we can stand and argue there if you'd like. Judging by the look of the accident, the state of the car seat and his type of cry, I'm pretty sure he's not injured. But I still need to check."

She felt her lips curl into a smile again. He had this way of talking that her aunt would have referred to disparagingly as "a bit of cheek." But it wasn't rude. Not at all. It was more like he was constantly trying to lighten the mood just enough to reassure her that she didn't have to be afraid. It was comforting.

"Okay. Just don't try anything funny." She straightened her rucksack on one shoulder, slid the scissors into her belt and picked up Fitz's car seat with the opposite hand.

Max reached to pick up the flashlight and she saw the curve of a smile at the corner of his mouth. "I wouldn't dream of it."

She followed him back through the woods to his paramedic vehicle. Max ran the light over the back of it. The right rear fender looked like a giant hand had punched it.

"I'm sorry," she said. "I can give you some money to cover repairs and to pay for gas."

"Please don't worry about it," he said. "Now, if it's okay with you, I'd like to double-check that Fitz is every bit as healthy as we both think he is."

She nodded and set the car seat down. She hadn't managed to salvage the toy boat Gerry had thoughtfully bought his son. But Fitz had somehow managed to pull the soft yellow fabric sail off and now clutched it to his cheek like a blanket. "Max is going to take a quick look at you and make sure you're okay. Nothing to worry about."

She wasn't sure if she was reassuring Fitz or herself. Either way, she stepped back and watched as he approached, crouched down and gently brushed his fingers along Fitz's pudgy limbs. Fitz looked up at Max. His huge baby blue eyes filled with wonderment. Yeah, she knew how he felt.

"You're okay, aren't you, buddy?" Max said, softly. He reached into the car seat and carefully pulled Fitz out and into his arms.

Daisy's breath caught in her throat. Every muscle in her body tensed. The only other person she'd ever seen hold Fitz were those moments she left him and Gerry alone to open and play with whatever new toy he'd brought. Not even Anna had shown any interest in holding her stepson. Daisy always figured she needed time to warm up. Now she never would.

"Can you hold him?" Max asked. Without missing a beat, he slipped Fitz into her waiting arms even as she felt her hands reach out instinctively to take him. "I find with a child this small, a lot of caregivers are more comfortable if they hold him during an examination."

She watched and waited while Max carefully checked Fitz's eyes and ran his hands over his limbs. Fitz chortled, and his laughter made something catch in Daisy's throat.

"He's teething," she said. "Lower gum on the right side. He's been fussing more than usual and has a slight fever that comes and goes."

"All very normal." Max nodded seriously. Then he stepped back and checked the car seat over. "Everything seems fine. No sign of injury, trauma or distress. The fact the car seat didn't sustain any damage is a good sign. Still, you shouldn't reuse a car seat after it's been in an accident. But the rental place should have one and I do have a spare one in my vehicle we can use for now. Now, how about you? Any pain from the accident? How are you feeling?"

He looked at her pensively, like she was a bomb he needed to defuse or a problem he needed to solve.

"I'm fine," she said. "A bit stiff and sore, but I'll live. Now, tell me, why are you doing this?"

He paused. There was no smile on his face now. But even with a slight frown, there was still something soft about his face. "I told you. You're in trouble and you need help."

The moon disappeared behind the clouds. A shiver ran down her back. "I told you I didn't want your help."

"I know," he said. "But that doesn't mean you don't need it."

The rain fell suddenly, in just a few scattered drops like the splattering of a garden hose. Fitz screamed. Daisy wrapped her arms around him and ran for the shelter of the truck. Max opened the back door for her, and she climbed onto the back seat and held Fitz on her lap while Max ran back around to get the car seat.

She looked around the vehicle. She'd thought it was a police vehicle when she'd first passed it. Now she saw it was actually a truck, with both a front and a back seat. The covered truck bed was filled with brightly colored and neatly stacked bags of medical equipment, with labels like Primary Response, Secondary Response and Pediatric. The front of the unit had a laptop, a huge screen and some kind of radio device.

Fitz squealed happily and tried to lunge between the seats to push the shiny buttons. She caught him. "I think Fitz wants to play with your toys."

Max laughed. "I don't blame him. I've got some pretty snazzy gadgets." He leaned in the opposite door and strapped the car seat in.

"What is this thing you're driving anyway?" she asked. "I thought it was a police vehicle at first."

"A rapid-response unit can do everything an ambulance can do except transport an injured person to hospital," Max said. Raindrops brushed the strong lines of his jaw. He clipped the seat belt in place around the car seat, then pulled it carefully, checking each strap in turn. "Think of it like this, if you get into an accident, a rapid-response vehicle will probably get there first, then an ambulance if needed. Or, if neither can reach you, we'll send in an air-ambulance helicopter, which happens a lot around here."

"Do you ever fly the helicopter?" she asked.

"I fly *in* the helicopter, but I don't pilot it," he said. "I do know how to fly a helicopter, though. I've taken enough piloting lessons. I've just never tested for my pilot's license."

"Why not?" She felt her nose crinkle. "If I could fly something, nothing would stop me."

He stepped back as if something about her comment surprised him.

She slid across the seat and buckled Fitz in. Then she ran around to the passenger-side door as Max opened it for her. Now she could see there was a full computer keyboard mounted between the two front seats and a whole lot of red-and-brown takeout coffee cups on the floor.

He blushed and quickly swept the trash into a black garbage bag that he yanked out from somewhere under the seat. He waited until she got in and closed the door behind her, before running back around and getting in the driver's seat. He turned the ignition and pulled back onto the road.

"Usually people ask me the opposite question. Why did I train to fly a helicopter, considering paramedics aren't pilots?" he said after a long moment, and she wondered how much he'd been playing her question around in his head.

"What do you tell them?" she asked.

"I tell people it's because I've got two older brothers," he said. "Trent and Jacob are eight and ten years older than me. I grew up chasing after them and trying to prove I could do whatever they could do, while always suspecting they looked at me like the annoying little brother who couldn't keep up. Sitting in the helicopter while some other man or woman flies me around irked me. It felt too much like getting my brothers to drive me around places in the family car. I have this weird independent streak."

"I left home at sixteen and had hiked around most of Britain and Europe by the time I was twenty-one," she said. "I think I can beat you when it comes to independence."

"I didn't think it was a competition, but if it is, then you win!" He laughed and ran his hand over his head. "I don't have a good answer as to why I never got my pilot's license. Maybe because I'm very happy with how my life is right now and don't want someone getting the bright idea I should make a career shift. Or maybe I've just always hated tests and competitions. Like, really hated them. Turning things from fun to serious ruined them for me.

"When I was a kid, my dad built this huge

shooting-and-paintball range in the woods behind our house. We all learned to shoot. Both Trent and my little brother, Nick, went on to enter competitions and win trophies and medals. I just shot for fun. Or maybe I was too clumsy and hated being showed up by my overly confident little brother. Nick's four years younger than me and he's got the cute-baby-of-the-family thing going for him. I didn't have that advantage."

Oh, she didn't know about that. Max seemed plenty cute from where she was sitting. He cut her a sideways glance, a casual and slightly wry grin slid across his mouth and something in his eyes sparkled.

She felt a sudden heat rise to her face. None of this was personal. He was only making conversation to ease her fears. He had to be. Yet, for a moment she caught a glimpse of the man he could be when there wasn't a gunman or crisis at hand. It was a nice look.

"No sisters?" she asked.

Then just as suddenly as it appeared, the light faded from his eyes. He turned and stared ahead through the windshield, his hands tightened on the steering wheel at exactly ten and two. A frown crossed his mouth and his head shook slightly.

Okay, so she'd take that as a no.

Or at the very least, a no comment.

Silence filled the vehicle, punctuated by the occasional squeak of the windshield wipers as they wiped away the intermitted sprays of rain.

"As you've probably guessed, I'm English," she said, after a long moment. "This is my first trip to Canada and I've done absolutely no sightseeing. Literally all I've seen is Fitz's house and some highway. But I've traveled all around Europe and the UK. Even a bit of the Middle East and northern Africa. I grew up in this really tiny town where everybody knew everybody. I have four half siblings, but they're all a lot younger than me. My stepfather and I never got on, so I left home at sixteen and moved in with my aunt. I finished school early, got a childcare diploma and traveled a lot. Then I started working for a temp agency. Turned out being a nanny was a great job to have for someone who liked traveling."

She wasn't quite sure why she was telling him all that. Maybe it was because she wanted him to know that there was more to her than some helpless person he'd picked up from the side of the road. She was tough and, yeah, she was probably a couple of years younger than he was, but she'd lived.

Not that it really mattered what he thought of her. He'd be gone from her life in an hour.

She waited until he seemed lost in thought, slid her rucksack open and ran her thumb slowly over the stack of hundred-dollar bills, tilting her bag so Max couldn't see in. They were wrapped together so tightly she could barely wiggle one out with her fingers. Why would Gerry have that much money just lying around in his car? Was it emergency money? Did he know she'd have to run with Fitz?

She pulled out the cell phone that she'd found with the money and turned it on. It asked for a password. She turned it off again, dropped it back in the bag and leaned back against the seat. So much for her idea of using it as a backup phone.

Gerry had texted exactly twice on the phone he'd given her when she'd fled. The first was a very long text, telling her that Anna had died, but that he was fine and recovering from smoke inhalation in a Montreal hospital. He added that she should be very cautious but that he was hopeful he'd get a good and trustworthy cop to meet up with her en route. His second text was just two words long: How's Fitz?

At the time, she'd texted back that he was fine and that she was making good time. But that was before the accident. Now she wasn't sure what to tell him or when.

It was almost two o'clock in the morning now. Surely, Gerry would be asleep. Either that or dealing with enough other worries. But the guilt of worrying him with the news that his son had been in an accident was less than the guilt of not telling him. Her phone was down to just one bar of cell signal that kept flickering in and out.

She wrote him a very short text, with the bare minimum of information and the repeated assurance that Fitz was fine. The message-sending symbol circled before finally giving her a bright red alert that the text hadn't gone, but the phone would try to send it again when it got a better signal.

She leaned her head back against the seat and prayed she'd be able to text him that they were back en route soon.

She glanced at Max. His brow was crinkled.

"What are you thinking about?" she asked.

"Fitz's mother," Max said. He frowned. "I'm sorry, it's an occupational hazard. Your comment raised a medical question, and now I want to know an answer. I promised I wouldn't pry and I mean it. But you told me that she died in childbirth. And the statistical likelihood of that happening is about one in ten thousand babies born in Canada. I've delivered my fair share of roadside babies, and I've never lost one yet. So I'm wondering what her specific complications were or if they're congenital."

"I have no idea," she admitted. The phone Gerry gave her buzzed. She glanced at the screen. It was a new text from an unknown number.

Hello, Daisy.
A friendly word of warning. Do not underestimate the people who are out to steal Fitz or what they'll do to get their hands on him. Trust no one. Anna Pearce intentionally sabotaged your work-visa paperwork. That means you're here illegally. If you go to police, you will be arrested; you will be deported; Fitz will be taken and you'll never see my little boy again.
Jane.

Daisy's hand rose to her lips as horror swept over her heart. Jane was Fitz's birth mother.

And she was dead.

THREE

Max's head turned as a gasp slid from Daisy's lips. Her face had gone so pale his brain immediately snapped into diagnosis mode. "What's wrong?"

She shook her head. "Don't worry about it."

Right, a woman who was clearly in danger looked on the verge of having an actual panic attack on the passenger seat of his paramedic vehicle and he wasn't supposed to worry about it.

God, I could use some pretty heavy-duty guidance here. I don't know what to say or how to help her. Let alone any clue how to do this hero thing.

A diner loomed to their right, with the lights off and a big sign at the front of a huge lot saying that it would open again for the summer in June. A few minutes later, a wooden sign welcomed them to Bleak Point, Algonquin.

It was the kind of town that was so small most tourists wouldn't even notice, except for the brief speed limit change. It had a smattering of houses, two gas stations, a grocery store and a sad little motel that had a single light on and advertised twenty-four-hour service, a convenience store and holiday cabins. A faded sign for a recognizable car-rental chain hung at the town's only mechanic.

His heart sank. It wasn't surprising that a small town in cottage country had a car-rental place. But he'd been half hoping that Daisy wouldn't be able to rent a car, giving him a perfect excuse to take her all the way with him to Hunstville. He could drop her at his parents' farmhouse where his folks would make a fuss over Fitz, she'd be able to get some sleep and he'd be able to call his brothers for advice.

Her forehead wrinkled. "Five hours until I can rent a car."

"Or we can keep driving," he said. "We're only two hours from Huntsville. It's a much larger small town. I know for sure you'll be able to rent a car there."

She didn't answer. Instead, she just glanced at her phone, back over her shoulder to Fitz, and then back at her phone again. "No, it's okay. Please just drop me off at the motel."

"But it's no trouble," he said. "I told you Huntsville is my hometown. I'm going there anyway."

"Thank you." Her chin rose as her arms crossed. "But you've done more than enough. I'll rent a cabin, feed Fitz and maybe have a quick a nap, if he'll agree to sleep. I've been awake since seven o'clock this morning."

So over twenty hours, then. She must be beyond exhausted. The temptation to lecture her on all the ways her body and faculties would be compromised if she didn't sleep soon flickered in the back of his mind. Instead, he turned the vehicle around and drove to the motel. The desire not to leave her there gnawed in the pit his stomach. Instead, his eyes rose to the dark sky above.

God, what do I do? I can't just take off and leave them here. But she doesn't want my help.

And it wasn't like he wanted to get messed up in somebody else's problem either. He had no clue how deep this rabbit hole went. He wasn't an undercover detective like his brother Trent, who spent months carefully unraveling a problem. Not at all. Swoop in, save someone from danger, make sure they were safe and then move on—that was how he liked it and why he preferred driving a rapid-response unit over an ambulance.

They reached the motel. A long low building with a small convenience store stood at the entrance of what a peeling wooden sign optimistically called a holiday camp. A light glowed dimly in the window and a sign told them to ring the bell for service after hours. He parked and waited while Daisy got out and opened the door to the back seat. She paused there for so long he almost wondered if she was rifling through his things. He glanced back.

"If you're looking for your car seat," he said. "Please don't worry about it and take mine. The car rental place might not have a good one. I'll give you my number, and after you're sorted and safe, you can give me a shout and we'll figure out a way for you to get it back to me."

Her dark eyes watched his face for a long moment. Her lower lip quivered ever so slightly, like she was fighting the urge to frown.

Realization hit him between the eyes. She would never call him. She would never try to track him down. He'd never find out the full story of the beautiful and brave English nanny who was on the run for her life, protecting the small baby in her care. She didn't say a word of that out loud, though. She didn't have to. He could read it in her face. When she said goodbye, it would be forever.

"That's very kind of you," she said. "Thank you."

"I'll wait here to make sure you're able to rent a place," he said quickly before she could say anything more. "I don't want to leave until you're sorted."

"Okay, thanks." She unbuckled the car seat, slung her rucksack over one shoulder and picked up Fitz with the other hand. He watched as she walked up to the front door and rung the bell. A couple of minutes ticked past and then a young man who didn't look much older than eighteen opened the door. Daisy carried Fitz inside.

Max let out a long sigh, like he'd been holding his breath since he'd watched her car fly past. What was he doing? He hadn't seen another glimpse of the gray sedan or any other suspicious driver since the accident, which hopefully meant the mysterious Smith had moved on.

Either way, just how long was Max going to follow her around, watching her back like some kind of knight in blue waterproof armor?

He pulled out his phone. It had one bar of signal and that would have to be enough. He dialed Trent, praying he'd be forgiven for waking him up at three in the morning.

"Detective Henry." His older brother's voice was on the line, confident and assured, before it could even ring once.

"Morning, bro." Max hopped out of his vehicle, beyond thankful his brother was answering his phone. "Sorry to call at such a horrible hour. I'm stuck in a pretty bad situation. I don't know what to do."

"No worries," Trent said. "Chloe and I are just sitting in my car on a stakeout, and we're about out of interesting small talk about wedding details."

He heard Chloe snort. Max smiled. *Thank You, Lord!* His brother Trent was amazing. But Chloe was a decorated detective with the Ontario Provincial Police's special victims unit, an expert in dealing with female crime survivors and one of the strongest women he'd ever met—which she had to be to marry a man like his brother. Both an RCMP detective and an OPP detective in one call? Perfect. "Can you put me on speakerphone? I'd love to get her take, too."

"Sure thing," Trent said. There were some

muffled sounds as Trent filled Chloe in. Max glanced toward the office and watched through a gap in the curtains as Daisy exchanged three of Canada's golden-colored hundred-dollar bills for a key on a string. His brow furrowed. That was a lot of spare cash for anyone to be carrying, let alone someone on the run. Daisy disappeared from view in the direction of the convenience store. The young man followed.

"Hey, Max!" Chloe's voice came on the line, along with the unmistakable background speakerphone hiss. "You've got us both now. What's going on? Anything's got to be more interesting than staring at a warehouse."

"I need to talk to you informally as family," he said, "not in your official capacity as police."

"Understood," Trent said.

"I... There's... Well, I met this woman..." Okay, so this was coming out all wrong. He paused, took a deep breath and reminded himself to keep it short and simple. Both Trent and Chloe were experienced cops and just as used to getting incident reports as he was to giving them. He leaned back against his vehicle and mentally switched his brain into paramedic mode. "Correction. I witnessed an accident on the highway. Intentional collision. I was the sole witness. A man in a gray car with flashing interior lights struck a woman in a sports car. His vehicle appeared to be that of an undercover cop, but he himself didn't appear to be one and did not produce a badge when requested. The woman had a baby in the car. I stopped. No visible injuries to either woman or child. He pulled a weapon on her. I intervened. He left."

There, not quite in chronological order, and nothing about the unusual impact Daisy seemed to have on his brain, but all the pertinent information was there.

He heard Chloe take in a breath. "Where is she now?"

"Her vehicle was totaled, so I drove them both to Bleak Point. It's a tiny dot on the map just south of Algonquin Provincial Park. She's currently renting a cabin and plans to rent a car in the morning. I'm standing outside the main office of the cabin rental place right now waiting for her. She also told me the baby's stepmother was murdered and the father asked her to take the baby somewhere. But I have no independent verification of those facts, and she refuses to supply any pertinent details. She's also determined not to involve police."

Neither his brother nor Chloe spoke. Though

something in the silence left him with the distinct impression that Trent wanted to ask a dozen questions and his future sister-in-law was making him wait.

"Look, I know I should call 911," Max added. "I'm not an idiot. But it's the middle of the night and she was standing in the woods with an infant. My highest priority was getting her to safety and trust me, she was not beneath either running or stabbing me with scissors. I don't know how to explain it. She's this tiny little thing, with long blond hair and a British accent, like something from the cover of one of Mom's books. But she's tough, like no one I've ever met, and very determined to get back on the road and take the baby wherever she's going. She hasn't asked me for help. She hasn't asked me for anything. But something about just walking away and leaving her here doesn't seem right. Not going to the police feels wrong, but going to the police when she's asked me not to also feels wrong."

There was a long pause. Chloe spoke first.

"First off, even if you call the police that doesn't mean she'd talk to them," Chloe said. "Crime victims refuse to cooperate all the time. You could've driven her right up to the closest OPP station and walked her inside, only to have her refuse to confirm anything you told them or say it had all been lies, and they'd be helpless to do anything. Police can't exactly force someone to give a statement when they don't want to. It's also possible she has an arrest warrant out for her or she's had a bad experience with police in the past and she's worried they won't do anything but make her life worse. Yes, she probably needs help. But you can't rescue someone who doesn't want to be rescued."

"Do you have any proof that the baby isn't hers or that anything she's telling you is true?" Trent asked. "She might just be running from a bad boyfriend and made up a fake story to get your sympathy. If so, it's also possible this guy in the car was a cop and didn't show a badge because he didn't want to get in trouble for what was basically a domestic-assault situation."

Well, weren't they doing a good job of making him doubt himself on everything. There was movement behind the glass. By the looks of things, Daisy was on her way back. Along with the baby in the car seat and the diaper bag, she'd added a large, disposable plastic bag to her load. "I've got to go. I think she's coming."

"Quickly," Trent said. "Tell me all the facts

you've got. Names, even if they're partial. Vehicle makes and models. Description of the suspects."

"Her name is Daisy," Max said, not that he liked anyone thinking of her as a suspect. "She's from England. The baby's name is Fitz. She called the gunman Smith. No second names for any of them. She said Fitz's stepmother was recently murdered by Smith, Fitz's mother had died in childbirth and she was acting on instructions from Fitz's father."

The door opened. Daisy stepped out and started toward him. He covered the phone with his hand and rattled off what he could remember of the cars' makes, models and license plates.

"Who are you talking to?" Daisy said. She crossed the driveway to where he was standing. Suspicion filled the darkness of her eyes as they narrowed.

"Gotta go, happy wedding planning," Max said quickly and hung up. Then he turned to her. "I was talking to my older brother Trent. He works really weird hours."

She watched his face. He waited, praying she wouldn't ask any more questions. Instead, she rubbed her eyes. They were red. He slid his phone into his other hand and reached out toward her. "You look exhausted. Can I help you carry something to your cabin?"

She hesitated. His phone buzzed. He glanced down, saw a text alert from Chloe and scanned it quickly while tilting it to shield it from her view.

Trent got a hit. He thinks she's a witness in a major organized-crime investigation. We need to get her and bring her in. We're coming to you. We'll be there in 6 hrs. Don't tip her off! Don't let her out of your sight!

Exhaustion dragged on Daisy's legs with every step. Her eyelids sank treacherously, threatening to close. Even with the restless nights of dealing with Fitz's teething cries and the Pearces' arguing, she couldn't remember ever going this long without sleep.

She wasn't exactly sure what to make of the fact that Max still hadn't left. But if she was totally honest with herself, she wasn't exactly looking forward to Max leaving, as much as she hated the thought of putting his life in danger.

They walked side by side up the winding dirt path through the trees and the smattering of deserted cabins. Thick woods lay to one side. A steep slope ran down to a dark and silent lake on the other. When the young man in the front office had pointed to a map, told her they were all empty and asked her which one she'd wanted, she'd instinctively chosen the one closest to the water and farthest from the road. Seems she'd underestimated just how far a walk that was.

Max shone his flashlight over the rocks and roots that jutted across the path. The smell of damp earth hung heavy in the spring air, mingled with hard patches of dirty ice that hadn't managed to thaw from winter. He made awkward small talk about the weather, none of which even began to explain why he was sticking around.

She cast little sideways glances at him, trying not to let herself notice how the light seemed to accentuate the rugged lined of his form and the softness of his eyes. Was he worried about them? Did he feel he had some obligation to her because he'd plucked them from an accident at the side of the road?

Her phone buzzed in her pocket, and she glanced at it. Her text to Gerry had gone through and he hadn't texted back yet, although any rational person would be asleep at this hour.

But it was that single text signed Jane from the blocked number that filled her heart with dread. The only Jane she knew of was Fitz's mother. The only Jane she knew was dead. Was this someone's idea of a sick joke? Had Jones got ahold of her number? Or Smith? Someone else?

She didn't know what to make of any of it and her exhausted brain was too tired to formulate a coherent guess. But something about the thought that Anna had intentionally sabotaged her visa paperwork as some kind of blackmail or threat to hold over Daisy's head rang undeniably true. It was the kind of thing the woman would've done, and it added an extra twist of malice to every time she'd told Daisy she was free to leave.

But now Anna was dead. The Pearces' country house was gone. Gerry was in the hospital.

If Daisy went to the police about any of it, she'd be arrested and deported, and she'd never see Fitz again. Hot tears threatened to fall from the corners of her overtired eyes. She refused to let them. The last thing this situation needed was Max thinking she was helpless. Max seemed to be one of the few genuinely nice guys in the world. He didn't deserve to get caught up in her mess.

"Well, here we are, number twenty-six," he said, far more cheerfully than the peeling wooden shack with its torn screen door deserved.

She forced the key into the knob of a door that looked like it had been kicked at more than once. She pushed the door open. They stepped inside, and she heard Max suck in a breath as the stench of years of neglect and filth filled their nostrils. She reached for the light.

The carpet was stained. A large, heavy television with rabbit ears sat in one corner of the living room, doubling as a coffee table. A small folding table and two metal chairs sat under a window, covered by faded curtains printed with barnyard animals. Through a door, she could see a single bed that had seen better days. But the kitchenette had a calcified kettle, hot plate and some mismatched dishes. It was a start. She set Fitz's car seat down on the table and then locked the door and slid the chain lock in place.

"You can't stay here," Max said. "There's got to be somewhere better you can go."

For a woman who was paying in cash and on the run? She doubted it.

"It's just for a few hours," she said. She didn't bother pretending to be cheerful and instead settled for determined. Yes, it was a bad situation. But she'd get through. She always did.

Fitz arched his back and fussed, a warning that it wouldn't be long until she had a full-on tantrum on her hands. Max glanced at his phone. She opened the container of liquid formula and poured it into one of Fitz's bottles, hoping that for once he wouldn't be picky about the brand and be willing to drink it cold. She nudged it into his hands. "Here, how about you try this for me, okay?"

Fitz batted the bottle away so quickly that it flew from her hand, hit the floor and rolled. Now was not the time for this. Then he looked up at her and whimpered. His lip quivered.

Her heart melted. Poor little thing. His mother and now his stepmother were both dead. His house had gone up in flames, and his life was in chaos. She wished there was something more she could do to put the pieces of his shattered world together for him.

"Hang on, okay?" her voice dropped. "Please just give me five minutes. I know this has been a rough day for you as well as me. I just need a moment to heat up the water, and then I'll make you some formula just the way you like it, okay?"

His face scrunched. Quickly, she lifted him out of his car seat. The moment he started screaming, it would take ages to calm him down.

"Let me hold him, please." Max slid his phone into his pocket. "Just long enough to calm him down and give you a break."

She pressed her lips together. Her limbs ached with a weariness that seemed to go right through them to the bone. She was so tired even the ugly mattress in the other room or the dirty carpet on the floor looked tempting enough to lie down on.

"I've delivered several babies," Max added. "I'm proficient in infant CPR, and I've rescued more tiny little lives than I can possibly count. I took the Red Cross babysitting course in high school and I've managed to hold him once already without dropping him. I'm just going to stand here and bounce him while you make him a bottle."

Fitz whimpered louder. His eyes looked up plaintively from Daisy to Max and back again. Something pulled at her heart like a thread tied somewhere deep inside her chest. The sudden weight of every decision she'd made in the past few hours and still had to make pressed down on her so heavily she had to gasp to breathe.

Lord, I'm scared. I'm lost and tired. I don't know why Max is still sticking around. I don't want him to leave and I'm not sure he should stay. Fitz has been my whole world these past few months, and it feels like I'm the only one who really loves him or who is looking out for his safety. Please help me be wise and protect Fitz.

"Okay," she said. "That would be a big help. Just don't try to leave or anything."

"Of course not." Max nodded solemnly. "I'll stay right here where you can see us."

He stretched out his hands. She eased Fitz into them, letting Max pull him from her grasp. Max cuddled him against his strong broad chest. Fitz looked up at him, eyes wide.

"Hey, little man." Max's voice dropped, soft and husky. He bounced him gently. "Now we're going to hang out while Daisy gets your food ready, okay?"

She turned back to the bottles and formula as sudden and unexpected tears rushed to her eyes. She'd never heard anyone else talk to Fitz that way. Anna had had no interest in him and whenever Gerry was around, he seemed uncomfortable with any contact with his son that didn't involve the exchange of gifts.

Her palms braced against the counter. She'd

never cared about anyone or anything quite the way she cared about that little baby. Even though protecting him from whatever big bad unknown threat was lurking out there in the darkness seemed even more impossible than ever.

She splashed some cold water on her face and then took a quick drink, before filling the kettle. The handle was cracked but the button glowed red when she plugged it in. She spread the meager contents of her grocery bag out on the counter while she waited for it to boil, took a bite of one of the plain teething cookies she'd bought for Fitz and chewed it without really tasting it. She carefully mixed and stirred the formula once the water had boiled, set it on the table to cool and then dropped down on the couch.

Her eyes closed before she could think to stop them. She quickly forced them open again, but not before Max had noticed.

"Why don't you nap for a few minutes?" Max said. "You really need to get some sleep and there's nothing like a teething baby to wreck anyone's ability to sleep. If it would help, I could bore you into unconsciousness by regaling you with details about all the negative impacts lack of sleep is probably having on your body and mind?"

The smile he gave her was almost as cheeky as Fitz's. Max was right. Fatigue dragged on her body like a current threatening to pull her under. She wouldn't be able to let herself sleep until Fitz was out himself. Thanks to his teething, she had no idea how long that would be or how long he'd let her sleep once he did. But the idea of napping while a stranger held Fitz was absolutely unthinkable.

"I'm not going to sleep," she said. "I'm just going to close my eyes while the bottle cools."

"I could give Fitz his bottle," Max said. "I'm an expert at squirting lukewarm formula on my wrist."

She stuck her tongue out at him and then blushed to realize she'd done something so silly. But he'd started it. Max laughed.

"I'm not going to close my eyes that long." She lay back against the couch and let her eyes close. Five minutes. That was all she'd allow herself. Then she'd give Fitz his bottle, thank Max for his help and then say goodbye.

She listened as Max pointed out the barnyard animals on the faded curtains to Fitz and made each animal's sound in turn. A smile curled on her lips. He was being ridiculous. But Fitz seemed to like it.

After a while, she heard a click and the slight hiss of static behind her, then a man's voice predicting intermittent showers. Sounded like Max had got the television going. Rain pattered on the metal roof. The television words faded, like the soft mumble of white noise.

"Breaking news. Police have issued a kidnapping alert for nine-month-old Fitz Pearce. The son of Quebec businessman Gerald Pearce was kidnapped following a massive explosion at the Pearces' country house outside Montreal in which at least one person died—"

"That's not true!" The words flew from her lips as her eyes jerked open, but even then, it took her brain a moment to catch up to the scene around her. Max was sitting in a chair by the window, with Fitz fast asleep in a ball on his chest. His eyes were grim. Instinctively her empty arms reached for Fitz. "Please let me hold him, and I'll explain."

Max didn't move. The empty bottle sat next to him on the table. Faint predawn light filtered through the curtains and the clock read quarter to six.

She'd been asleep for two and a half hours? She pushed herself to her feet, feeling her head swim, as her eyes focused on the television. She watched as a lavish photo of Gerry and Anna on their wedding day hovered above text about the mansion fire. Then her own face filled the screen.

"Police have issued a warrant for the arrest of the child's nanny, Daisy Hayward. Anyone with any information is requested to call Crime Stoppers."

A number rolled across the bottom of the screen. Any flicker of that smile she'd got used to seeing on Max's face was gone. Green eyes met hers, as cold and unrelenting as the edge of a knife.

"Fitz fell asleep on my chest," he said. "He drank his entire bottle, and then I changed him. His teething fever was back and he had a bit of a cough, so I was afraid if I put him down, he'd scream. His fever's gone back down again."

Instinctively her hands reached toward Fitz again. But Max didn't let her take him. Instead, one long leg stretched toward the metal folding chair opposite him. Gently, he kicked it out from the table and nudged it toward her.

"Sit," he said. "It's time you and I talk."

It wasn't a request. She couldn't sit. Her legs shook like they were full of adrenaline and needed to run. Instead, she paced.

"What the television said isn't true!" she said. "Yes, I'm Daisy Hayward, and yes, that's Fitz Pearce. But I didn't kidnap him! I'm trying to protect him. Some really bad people are after us and the longer you stick around, the more danger you'll be in. I don't want you involved in this."

"It's too late for that," Max said. "I am involved and I'm not going anywhere. So unless you want me calling 911 immediately and reporting that I've found a kidnapped child, you'd better start talking."

She took a breath, feeling an ache almost like cold spreading through her chest.

"I was putting Fitz to bed in the nursery last night when I heard shouting. I looked out the door and saw two of Gerry's guys trashing the place. One was Smith and the other is named Jones. He's almost like his equally evil twin brother. Then I heard a gunshot and saw Anna lying on the floor, dead. She didn't die in an explosion. She was murdered. Jones came after me. I grabbed Fitz and climbed out the window. Gerry pulled up and told me to get in his car and take Fitz to his place in Sault Sainte Marie. Jones fired. Gerry fired back. That was when the house exploded. I saw a cop car rush toward the fire. Then I drove for a long time and that's where you come in. That's all I know."

"That can't be all you know," he said. "Because it doesn't make sense."

"What difference does that make?" Her voice rose. The story had changed on the television but she smacked it off anyway. Then she yanked the phone Gerry had given her from her rucksack, opened it to Gerry's last message and slapped it down on the table in front of him.

He picked it up and read. Her gaze rose to the water-stained tiles above her head. A visceral memory swept over her of standing in her own living room back in England as a teenager, trying to make the big and strong men in uniform believe that even though they considered her retired-cop stepfather to be one of them, and even though everyone but her denied it, he really had struck her mother.

"I know how it looks. But just because something doesn't make sense doesn't mean it's not true."

Max closed his eyes, dropped his head in his hand and prayed out loud, "Lord, help me. What do I do?"

She heard the crack of footsteps outside. Quickly she turned and threw her weight against the door and double-checked both the doorknob lock and the chain lock, just as the door handle rattled. She glanced through the shabby peephole. Two hulking, bald figures stood outside the cabin door.

Smith and Jones had found them.

FOUR

Max watched as fear swept over Daisy's slender frame. Instinctively, he stood, stepped back against the far wall and held the still-sleeping Fitz tight to his chest, sheltering him in his arms.

"They've found me." Her voice barely rose above a whisper. Fear and panic etched the soft lines of her face. "Jones and Smith. They're here for Fitz."

"What? Are you sure?" He hadn't been able to see past her, and between the television alert and the doubts Trent and Chloe had stirred in his mind, he didn't know what to think. The only two facts he knew for sure were that they thought she was a witness to something involving organized crime and she'd been called a kidnapper on television. Could've been her rattling the doorknob to change the subject for all he knew, and now that she'd stepped back from the door, silence had fallen.

He glanced toward the window but couldn't see much of anything through the gaps in the barnyard-animal curtains. "I don't hear anything."

"That's because they're just standing there, listening!" she hissed. She gestured to the peephole, beckoning him to come across the room to look through it for himself. "Please, I'm begging you. Let me take Fitz, slip out the back window and run!"

Fitz squirmed in his arms. The baby was beginning to wake. "Look, Daisy, I want to believe you. I really do, but I can't—"

A loud knock shook the cabin door. It sounded like less of a greeting and more an attempt to see just how much punishment the door could take.

"Daisy, we don't want to hurt you." The voice was male and calm to the point of being cold. "Gerald just wants his son back. Just give him to us, and we'll go."

Fitz whimpered and Max felt him pull away from him and toward Daisy. But despite the very obvious connection he'd seen between those two, Fitz wasn't her baby. He belonged with his real family. And the truth of that burned through Max's limbs, shaking him to his core. He couldn't let this woman—no matter how captivating, beautiful or tender she was—just run off with a baby that she'd been accused of kidnapping.

"Don't be foolish!" Now the voice outside was laced with menace. "We know you're in there. Give us the baby, and you won't get hurt. A young woman like you all alone in a place like this with a stolen baby? So many terrible things could happen to you and nobody would be around to help you."

Oh, that man was wrong. He might know she was in there and think she was alone, maybe because she'd checked into the cabin by herself. Max had parked the rapid-response truck at the far end of the lot, far away from the road, where it wasn't likely to be seen by Smith should he return. But Daisy wasn't alone in this. She had him.

"Please, Max," Daisy begged, "let me take him and run."

Lord, what do I do? Trent and Chloe were at least two hours away and the closest police station was over an hour away. The bedroom window was wide, with sliding glass and a yellowed screen. If Daisy climbed through, he could pass Fitz to her and she could slip into the thick trees behind the cottage. But would she just run and never look back?

A swift kick knocked the door through the frame. It flew open, clattered against the chain lock and hung open. A large hand reached through and fumbled to unlock the chain. Daisy yanked the scissors from her belt and stabbed it. A voice bellowed and swore in anger. The hand disappeared back through the door. Daisy threw her weight against the door, slamming it hard.

"I'll give you to the count of three!" A second voice echoed through the door now, this one was louder, less controlled and most definitely belonged to the man named Smith. "Then I'm breaking down the door and taking what we came for."

Daisy's eyes turned to Max, brimming with vulnerability, determination and strength that took his breath away.

"Please," she whispered. "We can't let them take him. We just can't."

He didn't know much. But that much he knew.

"One!" Smith shouted.

Max shifted Fitz into one arm and reached out the other for Daisy.

"Come on," he said. "We'll both go out the bedroom window."

"Two!"

"Stay close." Max turned and ran through the doorway into the bedroom, tucking Fitz carefully and snuggly into the safety of the crook of his arm. Something buzzed in his hand and suddenly he realized he still had the phone Daisy had given him.

He glanced back. Daisy was gathering up everything they'd brought, as if trying to hide the fact Fitz had ever been there. Then she started digging through her rucksack like she was looking for something. What could possibly be in there that was so important she'd risk delaying for?

Max stuffed the phone deep into his pocket. In two steps, he'd crossed the tiny bedroom, yanked the window open and punched out the screen so hard it popped out of the frame and flew to the ground. The sound of a hard blow and splintering wood came from behind him. Seemed Smith had decided to skip the number three and just start kicking.

Max leaped up onto the bed, grabbed the window frame with his free hand and swung his leg through the window, sheltering Fitz with his chest. "Daisy! Hurry up!"

"One second!" she said. He heard the sound of scissors opening and closing, "I have a plan to slow them down!"

"What plan?" he yelled. She didn't answer. He just heard her running around the other room like she was throwing paper. The last thing they needed right now was another secret. Another crash sounded. The door couldn't take that much more punishment. "Forget it! We'll outrun them."

"They'll have guns, high-powered ones, and if they realize we're running, they'll shoot." Her face appeared at the bedroom door. Her fingers gripped the door frame so hard her knuckles had gone white. "Promise me that no matter what happens, you'll protect Fitz and not let anyone hurt him."

Was she really asking him this now? He was halfway out a window with a baby in his arms. "Of course! But nothing's going to happen. We're sticking together. And that's final."

A crash thundered through the cottage. Time to go. Max pushed through the bedroom window and landed on the wet grass below. He shifted Fitz around to his chest and sheltered him there as he dashed into the thick tree cover. Then he crouched behind a tree and looked back. The window lay there, open and empty, like an aching wound in the middle of the badly painted wall.

He stared at it, willing her to come through. Then a flash of blond filled his view and a prayer of relief filled his chest as Daisy vaulted through. Her slender limbs tensed as she landed on the grass below. She glanced up, uncertain, as she searched for him in the foliage. Then her eyes met his. A determined smile crossed her lips. She leaped up and sprinted toward him, and he felt his hand reach out to hers.

A gun blast shook the air. A large bald man with facial scars was running toward her, around the back side of the cottage. Daisy sprinted for the tree line. He raised the gun and fired again. The bullet flew over her head and crashed through trees, shredding pine branches above Max's head and he felt his heart begging her not to stop.

"If you keep running, I'll keep shooting!" bellowed the man whom Max guessed was Jones. "I don't care if I've got to tear the whole forest to shreds to hit you."

Daisy stopped and Max watched as a cry of defeat slipped through her lips. She dropped to her knees, suddenly, inches from the tree line. Her hands rose above her head. "Stop shooting! I surrender."

What was she doing? Daisy's eyes met his through the branches. Her delicate lips moved in one single, silent, unmistakable word: *Run.*

He got it, with a sickening certainly that hurt something inside him. If she ran and Jones kept firing, Fitz could be found or shot by a stray bullet. But if she stayed behind... If she bought him time...

Daisy, no! He couldn't just save Fitz and let her get taken and hurt by those men. There had to be another way. Max scanned the wet ground, as the hopeless thought of somehow finding somewhere safe to leave Fitz so he could go back and help Daisy filled his foolish heart. But Daisy shook her head, as if she could read his mind and was pleading with him not to risk Fitz's life to save hers.

Suddenly he saw in a flash of aching clarity that, while there might be a whole lot of things he didn't know or understand, there was one more thing he knew for absolute certain— Daisy loved Fitz. So much that she was willing to die to keep him safe.

He felt Fitz's tiny hand grab his shirt and clutch it tightly. Max held him close. Daisy closed her eyes and turned away from him.

"Where's the baby?" Jones walked toward her.

"A paramedic took him."

Max watched, helpless, as Jones raised his weapon to her head and pressed the barrel between her eyes. "Where is he taking him?"

Her voice rose, loud and defiant. "I honestly don't know. He didn't tell me."

Then as Max watched, the gun flew hard at the side of her head. She crumpled to the ground.

Pain pulsed through Daisy's head, filling her vision with nothing but flashes of light on a backdrop of inky black, blocking out her ability to think. She hit the ground and lay there, her eyes closed and lungs gasping. But the feeling in her body was nothing compared to the visceral ache in her chest.

Fitz was gone. Max had taken him. She didn't know if she'd done the right thing or if she'd ever see Fitz again. All she knew was that it hadn't been a choice. The moment she'd heard the gun firing into the woods, she'd known there was only one thing she could do. She had to get Jones to stop firing. She had to do whatever it took to let Fitz live, even if it meant letting Max take him.

She kept her eyes closed. Sudden tears pressed against her lids as her mind filled with the memory of Max cradling Fitz in his strong and muscular arms. The look in his eyes as he'd gazed down at Fitz had been so tender and caring. He'd radiated comfort and protection in a way no one ever had before, which had made it cut all the deeper to see the doubt and suspicion in his face and know just what he thought of her. He believed she was a liar and a criminal.

Lord, I have to hope that despite how little he thinks of me that my instincts about him are right. That he is a good man who believes in You and will keep Fitz safe.

Jones grabbed her legs and dragged her across the wet grass away from the forest. Away from where Max and Fitz had run. She stayed limp and let him take her. She'd save her energy for when she could escape, and she had to believe that she would. In the meantime, every moment Jones and Smith were distracted with her bought Max another moment to get away. Voices floated above her in the darkness.

"There's sugar maple money spread all over the cabin," Smith said. "Hundreds and hundreds of it. Everywhere."

She'd never heard Canadian hundreds referred to as *sugar maple money* before, but they could call it whatever they wanted as long as it bought Max time to get away. In those precious seconds when he had run for the window with Fitz in his arms, she'd realized there was only one thing she could think of that would slow them down—money. So she'd slid the wrapper off the two wads of bills and scattered them all around the cabin before stuffing a few in her bag.

Yes, she'd lose thousands. But it was Gerry's money, and she'd only been using it to care for Fitz. If Smith and Jones caught her, they'd find it anyway and no amount of money was worth Fitz's life.

She just had to hope that Max eventually found the two hundred-dollar bills that she'd slipped into the pocket of the black leather jacket he'd had lying in the back of his truck. He'd refused to take money from her to cover repairs and she'd figured he'd find it eventually and smile, knowing it was from her. Now, she was just thankful he had it to help take care of Fitz.

"You're kidding me!" Jones whistled. "This I gotta see."

"Wait," Smith said. "Where's the baby?"

"She doesn't have him. She said a paramedic took him."

Smith swore. Rough hands yanked the backpack off her arms. She heard someone shaking the contents out onto the ground.

"More money. Baby stuff. A burner cell phone." Smith sounded hopeful for a moment. Then he swore. "It's locked."

"I'm going to go search the cottage," Jones said.

"There's no baby there!" Smith shouted. "There's not even any evidence a baby was ever there! Why is she just lying there?"

"She's passed out!"

"No, she's not," Smith snarled. Then came pain, sharp and relentless, as Smith stomped hard on her knee. A cry slipped from her lips and she sat up, her eyes wide. Smith chuckled.

She looked up at them as they stood over her, menacing and huge, and she wondered if this was what Anna had seen right before they'd killed her. Who were they really, and what were they really after? If they worked for Gerry, then why had they killed Anna and set fire to the house?

"Where did the money come from?" Smith barked.

"Gerry's car!" she said quickly.

"Where did the paramedic take the baby?" Jones asked.

"I have no idea!" she cried, knowing the

best alibi was the truth. "He saw an alert on the news saying I'd kidnapped Fitz!"

"And he left you with thousands of dollars?" Smith leaned down.

"He's a good man, and he didn't know anything about the money." Her hands rose and she let them shake in a sign of submission, as every ounce of the genuine anguish and uncertainty she felt seeped through her words. "After you crashed into me and totaled Gerry's car, Max chased after me and insisted on giving me a ride. I went with him. You'd wrecked my car, what other choice did I have? When he heard I had a warrant out for my arrest, we argued and I begged him not to call the police. I don't think he believed much of what I said."

Every single word of which was true and scared her in a vein-deep way that coursed through her core.

"She's just some idiot girl," Jones said, looking at Smith. His head shook in disgust. "She doesn't know anything. She only got this far because she stumbled into someone who helped her."

"I say we kill her, gather up the money and then go find the baby." Smith aimed his gun at her.

"No, we take her and use her as leverage."

"What leverage?" Smith snapped. "She got the money from Gerry. The paramedic has the baby. You really want to drag her around with us?"

"You want to risk somebody finding her body?" Jones countered. "Or you want to waste time hiding it? What happens when the guy who booked her this cabin sees her face on television and calls the police? They're going to come up here looking for her. They'll search the trees and dredge the lake. They'll probably bring dogs. If they find her body, they'll know somebody else has the baby."

"Okay, fine! We take her, we kill her and we drop her somewhere more isolated." Smith leered at her and leaned in closer. The barrel of the gun floated just a foot away from her face. "Well, girlie, looks like you're coming with us. So you'd better not give me any grief, because I'm going to have a nice long drive to decide just how I'm going to kill you."

She kicked up hard with all her might, catching him by the hand. Smith swore as the gun flew free from his fingers. He turned and ran for the gun.

She scrambled to her hands and knees and started running. Huge hands yanked her ankles back as Jones tackled her from behind.

She pitched forward, hit the ground and kicked back hard. Jones yelped and let go.

The gun fired behind her. Jones shouted, "Hey! Watch it! You could've killed me!"

She scrambled forward, throwing herself down the incline toward the lake. Bullets sounded over the air above her. Smith kept firing. Jones kept shouting. She rolled, letting her body tumble over the rocks and through brush. Then she hit the lake and sank into the frigid water.

Angry voices filled the air.

"Where did she go?" Jones bellowed.

"I don't know!" Smith yelled back. "You had her!"

"I think she jumped in the lake."

"And you expect me to jump in after her?"

She crawled forward on her hands and knees through the thick weeds and mud, prayers slipping through her mind and water stinging her skin numb. A metal storm drain loomed ahead of her. Water trickled out into the lake. She crawled inside and curled into a ball.

More gunfire was followed by more threats shouted in her direction and bitter arguing between the two men about whether or not to search for her or to just collect the money she'd scattered and go.

She stayed small, wrapped her arms around her legs and waited. The sun crept over the horizon. Water ran through the pipe by her feet. She prayed and listened as they rampaged around above her. Finally, voices faded into the distance. Silence fell. But still she stayed hidden and waited, as the sun rose through the trees and then filtered through the clouds.

She felt in her pocket for the phone Gerry had given her and only then remembered that Max had taken it. What was she going to do? Where was she going to go?

She waited as the sun rose higher in the sky, until it cast golden light shimmering on the lake. Then slowly and quietly, she crept out of the drainpipe and up the hill, expecting at any moment to hear cruel laughter and feel the harsh grip of hands grabbing her again. She stumbled up the bank and stood, muddy, soaked and cold.

"Max?" No answer. She crept toward the tree line where she'd seen him last and risked calling louder. "Max?"

Still no answer. Max was gone and so was Fitz.

Her bag and its contents, minus the money and electronic device, were strewed around the ground. She gathered them up. The door to the cottage lay open from where Smith and Jones had broken it down.

Daisy took a deep breath, slipped inside and surveyed the wreckage of the room where she'd stood, less than two hours ago, as the most handsome and compassionate man she'd ever met looked at her like she was some kind of monster.

The money was gone and the cabin was trashed. The bulky television that had called her a criminal had been smashed. The couch where she'd napped and the bed that she'd stepped on to climb through the window had both been sliced open with a knife. Handfuls of stuffing littered the ground.

She sat down on the edge of the ugly, sharp metal bed frame. Tears choked in her throat and memories of the precious baby boy she'd risked her life for swam in her mind's eye.

Now what, Lord? What do I do? Where do I go?

Faint chimes sounded outside. She got up and looked out, but there was no one there. She searched the ground and then her eyes scanned the trees, as the chimes sounded again. It sounded like a phone was out there somewhere, receiving text messages. She pushed through the woods and followed the sound.

Then she saw it. The cell phone that Gerry had given her was lying on top of an outcropping of rock wrapped in waterproof fabric, the same color blue of Max's paramedic uniform, as if he'd cut a strip from the cuff of his pants to keep the phone safe. She unwrapped the phone, expecting to see another message from Gerry.

Meet me at the diner on the highway. It will look closed, but the door will be unlocked.
　　Don't lose hope. It'll be ok. I promise.
Max

FIVE

Don't lose hope, Max thought, staring down at his phone, willing it to ring. He glanced out the diner window at the pale blue sky. Those three little words were such an easy thing to type, but much harder to do. He had no way of knowing where Daisy was or if she'd get the message. He didn't even know if she was still alive.

A chuckle drew his attention to his left. Fitz was sitting up in a diner high chair, smashing and smearing the remnants of a banana over the tray in between attempts at grabbing Max's cell phone.

Max didn't know exactly what connections Trent or Chloe had called in to get someone to show up and open the closed diner. He suspected it had something to do with the underground network of contacts they'd been working on to help trafficking and abuse victims find their ways home.

When he'd got a safe distance from the cabin, he'd doubled back to his vehicle and called Trent from the road. Chloe had called him back half an hour later with the news that someone with keys to the diner would meet him there to open it. It had been a woman in her late sixties, who'd brought a paper bag containing an egg sandwich for him, six homemade cookies, coffee, a banana and a bottle for Fitz.

She'd left without saying anything beyond telling Max to lock the door behind him. There'd even been a place behind the kitchen to shower and get changed into his civvies before attempting a quick catnap on the foldout cot while the baby slept.

Fitz stopped mashing and looked up at Max, his blue eyes suddenly worried and wide.

"Don't worry, buddy," Max said, softly. "I'm wondering where Daisy is, too. But she'll be okay."

His phone buzzed. The screen said the number was unknown. He answered it before it could finish ringing once. "Daisy?"

"No, bro, just us." Trent's voice crackled down the line with that familiar rumble of a car engine in the background that meant he was on speakerphone. "Chloe says we're about an hour away."

Wonderful. Max let out a long sigh of relief. "I texted her," he said. "Told her where I was and where to meet me. I don't know if she got the message, the battery was really low and the phone might even be dead. She might not have made it. Everything inside me wanted to run out there and fight for her. But they had guns, they were firing into the woods, and I couldn't risk Fitz."

"You did the right thing," Trent said. "You saved a child's life."

"Trent? If she dies, I'm never going to forgive myself."

"I get it," his brother said. "Better than anyone. You think I've never been put in the impossible situation of deciding whose life gets saved first? You want to remind me what WIN stands for?"

"What's Important Now."

"Right, and what's triage?"

Max couldn't believe his brother was trying to school him on his own job. "It means figuring out the most urgent thing and doing that first."

"Right," Trent said. "So trust yourself, trust

God and trust that together we're going to save both Daisy and Fitz. Have faith that Daisy is going to walk through that door. Then you're going to stall her until we can get there, make sure the baby's taken care of, bring Daisy in for questioning and hopefully resolve this whole situation before it escalates any further."

Bring her in. The words sat heavy in his gut. She'd looked him in the eyes and begged him not to call the police. Now, here he was, sitting in a trap that he'd helped two detectives bait.

Yes, he knew she'd told him she'd talk to the cops if she knew she could trust them. He also knew that she'd be safer with Trent and Chloe than she would be anywhere else. Yet, as Fitz went back to babbling happily and squishing banana, Max couldn't look him in the eye.

"She says she didn't kidnap him," Max told Trent. "She says Gerry Pearce told her to take him somewhere. I don't know why anyone would call in a kidnapped child alert or issue a warrant."

"Neither do I," Trent said. "But you have no idea how hard we're looking into things from our end. Without going into anything classified, I can tell you that a few months back, the vice unit was tracking a major organized-crimes case. Suddenly, a whole lot of evidence went missing. The electronic devices we still had were locked up tight with passwords our tech team still can't break, and I had reason to suspect that a couple of our cops had gone dirty. Sometimes, the people you think are clean just haven't hit their price yet. Bottom line is, it's not unreasonable for Daisy to distrust cops. In fact, if you are ever questioned by anyone in uniform about any of this, don't tell them I'm involved. We're dealing with some deeply classified stuff here."

Wasn't he always? Max nodded. "Got it."

"But that's big-picture stuff," Trent went on. "Right now, the priority is making sure that baby's okay. You didn't tip Daisy off, right?"

"No, of course not," Max said. "You told me not to. Also, I'm pretty sure if I had, she would've run. She practically begged me not to call the police—"

"You didn't call the police. You called your brother."

"Who just happens to be a highly respected undercover detective with the RCMP," Max said.

"Who got Daisy's case transferred to his jurisdiction," Trent countered. "Who has been working incredibly hard to get the warrant canceled and find out who called police and reported Fitz kidnapped."

"Just promise me you're not going to arrest her," Max said.

"I'm not in the habit of arresting people unless they commit a crime."

There was an edge to Trent's voice. It was straight shooting and controlled. Max wished he felt that way about any of this. Max's brothers often teased him about being unflappable, but it was easy to stay detached when he was running from one accident to another, without ever stopping or getting involved.

"I'm not joking," Max said. "I'm really not. Just promise me that you're not going to put her in handcuffs or something."

"I can't promise that, and you know it. Just like you can't promise she won't pull a knife or a gun or try to snatch the baby and run."

Daisy wouldn't do that! The desire to argue with his brother and to make him see just how special and different Daisy was rose up inside him like a wave. Trent hadn't seen the way she'd risked her life to save Fitz or witnessed the look in in her eyes.

Fitz chortled beside him, dragging Max's attention back to his wide enthusiastic grin, punctuated by little front teeth. His tiny fists waved.

Lord, why am I so wrapped up in this? I know Trent is right. I know he and Chloe have a duty to treat this like any other case. Why can't I?

The phone line beeped.

"Hang on," Trent said. "I've got a call coming in from a buddy in Organized Crime. Looks like someone has finally had his morning coffee. Hopefully, this will help us get some answers." The phone had gone dead even before Max could answer.

"Hey, Max." The sound of Daisy's voice made Max leap to his feet. He'd been so busy watching the front door he hadn't even stopped to think she could sneak in the back. She was standing in the doorway to the kitchen, soaking wet and covered in mud but somehow looking more beautiful than anything he'd ever seen before.

How long had she been standing there? How much had she heard?

"Who were you talking to?" she asked.

"My brother," he said, feeling his legs push him to his feet. "I… I can't tell you how wonderful it is to see you."

Suspicion needled at the back of his mind,

questioning how two armed killers just happened to let her go. But it evaporated as he watched Fitz laugh and reach out his arms for Daisy and heard the cry of relief burst through her lungs as she ran toward them. Max felt his arms open to catch her.

Instead she stopped short, a few inches away from the tip of his outstretched hand, scooped Fitz up from his chair and held him to her chest. Fitz squealed. She pulled the baby deeper into her arms.

Max turned away. What was she going to think when she discovered that he'd called Trent? What if Trent took Fitz away from her? How would she ever forgive him?

Then he felt a hand on his. Her fingers were slender, delicate even, and yet as they wove through his, their grip tightened with a strength that made something in his chest wish he'd never have to let her go.

"Thank you for keeping him safe."

"No problem," he said, feeling his own voice grow strangely deeper in his throat. "I'm so sorry I just left—"

"I told you to run." She tugged him closer. "I wanted you to save Fitz's life and you did."

Yes, but that didn't quell whatever it was that was beating in his heart and wishing he could've done so much more. He felt his arm slide along her back. His hand came to rest between her shoulder blades. Fitz reached out and grabbed the front of Max's shirt with his tiny hand, and Max let himself stand there for a long moment with one hand on her back, the other hand holding hers, and little baby Fitz nestled between them.

"Fitz and I had a good time hanging out," he said. "He's an amazing little guy. But I'm sure he's glad to be back with you." Max ran his fingers slowly over her arm, feeling the scrapes and bruises on her skin. "Some of these scrapes are pretty deep. We should get them cleaned up. I have a spray that should help. Do you have any other injuries I should know about? It looked like he knocked you out pretty bad."

"It looked worse than it was," she said.

His hand slid to her face and tilted her chin up so he could look into her eyes. "Tell me the truth, please. Did they hurt you?"

She shook her head. "Jones dragged me across the grass. Smith threatened to kill me if I didn't tell them where you'd taken Fitz. I kicked them both pretty hard, tumbled down the hill into the lake and hid. Then when they left, I found the phone and made my way here."

"You're incredible. You know that?" The words slipped from his lips before he could even think about whether they were the right or wrong thing to say. They were still standing so close that all he'd have to do was lean over Fitz's head and his lips would meet hers. The weird and unfamiliar lump in his throat grew heavier.

His phone began to ring again. "Sorry, that'll be my brother."

"No problem." She pulled away.

He glanced at the phone. Sure enough, the number was blocked. He declined the call, knowing Trent would wait a minute and call back.

"The formula I gave Fitz is on the counter," he said. "I don't know if it's the right brand, but I followed the instructions to the letter and he drank it. I don't think he ate any of the banana. He just mostly smeared it around, but he had fun. I parked my truck in the very edge of the parking lot and threw some camouflage netting over it, just in case Jones and Smith cruised the highway looking for a shiny white-and-yellow vehicle. Hang on, I'll give you my keys and you can go get my jump bag. It's bright red and has all the basic first-aid essentials anyone could ever need, including emergency food rations."

Max grabbed his leather jacket off the chair beside him and reached into the front pocket.

His fingers brushed his keys and suddenly he realized what he was about to do. She was a fugitive. Was he really about to hand her the means to escape, steal his vehicle and run away again? The keys hung from his fingers in the space between them.

Her eyes widened, then she looked around the diner as if realizing for the first time that he'd somehow managed to open a closed diner and procure food. Questions filled her eyes and he wasn't sure how he was going to answer them.

The phone started ringing. He needed her to trust him and to do that, he had to demonstrate that he was willing to trust her. Her fingers brushed his. He let his keys fall into her palm.

"I'll be back in a moment." She turned and walked out the back door, with Fitz in her arms. Max felt a long breath leave his lungs and only then realized he had banana on his shirt.

He answered the phone. "Hey! Sorry, I've only got a minute. She's here."

"Who's there, Mr. Henry?" The voice was female, slightly formal and exceedingly polite.

He took a step back. "Who is this?"

"A friend, Mr. Henry, someone who's trying to stop an unfortunate situation from spiraling any further out of hand than it already has and who wants to help keep you from making a huge mistake."

He gritted his teeth. "I'm not in the habit of taking advice from people who don't tell me their names."

"Don't be foolish!" In an instant, all pretense of politeness faded. "I could make up any name I wanted, now couldn't I? Call me Jane, if you want. It doesn't matter to me. You have no way of knowing if I'm telling the truth."

Heat rose to the back of his neck. He wasn't a spy, a cop or a detective. He dealt in unmistakable facts about what was broken and what was injured. That was how he saved lives. "What do you want?"

"I want the baby." At this, Jane's voice turned downright hard. "I want Fitzgerald Pearce the Second to be back where he belongs. That means getting him far away from Daisy Hayward. She's not the person you think she is. She's a criminal. She's been arrested for theft and charged with making false police reports. She lost her driver's license. If you turn your back on her, she'll rob you blind."

The heat had spread through his neck down his chest and now seemed to be burning through his veins, battling the cold wash of fear and uncertainty that Jane's voice sent shivering over his limbs. Was it his imagination or did he hear a car outside? He glanced out the front window but couldn't see anything.

"Tell me where you are." Jane's voice softened. "And I'll arrange to have someone come and collect him. That's all you have to do. Tell me where to find you, hand over the baby to me and you can turn around and walk away."

He turned back around. Daisy was standing in the back door with Fitz in her arms and Max's jump bag slung over her shoulder.

"Who are you, really?" His voice dropped to an urgent whisper. "How did you even get this number?"

Daisy was walking toward him now. Doubt pooled in her eyes. He turned away.

"Listen!" Jane's voice sharpened. "You're in danger! Don't you get that? This is not your problem. I'm trying to help you keep yourself from getting killed. Are you really ready to die for this woman?"

"Max?" Daisy's hand touched his shoulder. "Is everything okay?"

No, it really wasn't. Just how many secrets was he going to keep from her?

"A woman named Jane is on the phone." He turned toward her. "She's demanding we give her Fitz."

A gasp slipped from Daisy's lips. As he watched, the color drained from her face.

"Big mistake," Jane said. "You've just signed your own death warrant. I will find you, and I will get my hands on that baby. And if you try to stop me, what happens next is on you."

Fear spread down Daisy's limbs until she felt so numb she could barely even feel Fitz in her arms. *Jane.* The same woman who'd texted her and told her she'd be deported if she went to police?

Max growled at the phone, hung up and slid it back into his pocket. "So who's Jane?"

"I don't know…"

"Everything about your face right now says you're not telling me the whole truth." He crossed his arms, and everything about his face said that he was beyond frustrated and nearing fed up.

"I have no idea who you were just talking

to on the phone!" Her voice rose. "I got a text from someone named Jane last night. But the only person I know named Jane was Fitz's mother and she died in childbirth."

"Are you sure?" His eyes narrowed. "How old was she? Did she die in a hospital? Are there records? Was it a closed or open coffin at the funeral?"

"How would I know if there were medical records?" Daisy asked. "You think I have access to things like that? All I know for sure is what Gerry told me when I was hired and what I read in her obituary. Fitz was born in a Quebec hospital, I don't remember which one. Jane was in her early thirties when she died. Thirty-three, I think, so almost ten years older than Gerry's second wife but still a lot younger than him. Her cause of death wasn't in her obituary, and I never quizzed Gerry about it, because that would've been prying and it was not my place to ask. I'm his employee, not his friend. Most of what I know about their lives is what I've pieced together from scraps of arguments I've overheard. Anna and Gerry didn't exactly fight quietly, and they were having an affair long before Jane died. Why are you grilling me about her death?"

"Because I'm an emergency medical professional," Max said. "Like I told you last night. I've delivered babies, sometimes at the side of the roads from mothers who'd just survived accidents. I've not lost one yet. I'm not saying it doesn't ever happen, because I know as well as anyone how fragile life can be. But this whole story you're trying to sell me on, quite frankly, makes me feel like an idiot who can't tell when the pretty girl is pulling the wool over his eyes. You're the British nanny of a rich reclusive man who's had two wives die under mysterious circumstances—"

"I'm a licensed childcare professional, working for a successful computer engineer who lost his second wife in a violent home invasion!" she countered, ignoring the fact that Max sighed loudly. "Look, I'm being as honest with you as I can be! Whoever Jane is, she threatened me, too. She told me if I went to police, I'd be arrested."

"Arrested for what?" Max asked. His eyes darted to the window and she got the distinct impression he was watching for someone. "Is it true you lost your driver's license? Or that you were arrested for theft and filing false charges?"

She pressed her lips together. There was an intensity to the way he was interrogating her and almost a desperation behind his questions, like he was scrambling down a cliff and trying to grab onto anything that might stop his fall. "Honestly? She told me my boss didn't fill my work-visa paperwork properly, which means I'm not here legally, and if I'm arrested, I'll be deported and never see Fitz again."

"That didn't answer my question," Max said. "But that much I do believe. Because promising work visas but not delivering on them is exactly how criminals manage to traffic women overseas into low-paying jobs, and worse. I bet they also took your passport and tell you that they send all your pay home to your family in England. It's possible they chose you specifically because of that criminal record Jane said you have. Gerry wanted to make sure he could control you and you wouldn't go to police. That would make you a victim in all this."

He made it sound like that was a good thing. Like he was hoping to prove she was a victim. Like he was a trial lawyer preparing to argue her case just before they stepped through the courtroom door to face some relentless prosecution.

"Why are you talking like this?" She shook her head. "Gerry is not a crook and I am definitely not a victim."

Again his eyes darted to the window. "Tell me, was Jane right when she said you lost your driver's license?"

"What difference does it make?"

His eyes cut back to her face. "Please, Daisy, I need to know. Otherwise I can't help you."

Help her with what and against whom? "Yes, but I got it back—"

"Were you ever arrested?"

She felt her lip quiver and gritted her teeth to stop it. "Yes, but—"

"For theft and filing false charges?"

"Yes, both! But it was years ago, back home in England, long before I moved to Canada!" Her chin rose. Why was she bothering trying to explain herself to him?

Whatever was going on with him that had him so worked up, it was like he wasn't even listening. He was too busy throwing out loaded and misleading yes-or-no questions instead of just letting her tell the whole story, about how her stepfather once punished her by saying she'd stolen the car she'd bought from him and how he'd got some buddy on the police force to charge her with making false claims after she kept calling the police on the fact he'd got drunk and hit her mother. She hadn't been able to afford a lawyer, her mother had cried and begged her to plead guilty, telling her that if she did, she could move back home and because she was young it would be wiped from her record.

Her gut said no. Her instincts had told her to run. But she'd trusted her mother and pleaded guilty to crimes she hadn't committed. And instead, she'd been tossed back out on the street.

So that had been it for whatever it was inside her heart that had succumbed to her mother's tears. There'd be no more blind trust and no more trusting other people over her own instincts. That had been how she'd learned to never go down without a fight.

Max still hadn't spoken and just stood there looking at her like she was some problem he didn't know how to fix. Well, she didn't need him to fix her and she wasn't going to be his problem for very much longer.

"I don't know what to tell you," she said. "But I'm not just going to stand here and defend myself or play twenty questions. I don't owe you an explanation for my life, because quite frankly my life isn't any of your business. You saved Fitz's life and probably mine. I'm always going to be grateful for that. But it's clear you don't trust me and I have no reason to trust you.

"You think your behavior isn't incredibly suspicious? You're the one who is fielding calls from a dead woman who wants to turn you against me, was on the phone at three in the morning to your 'brother' and keeps hiding your phone every time you're on it like you're afraid I'm going to read your lips or glance at the screen. You're the one who broke into a closed diner and asked me to meet him there! How do I know you're not a crook?"

His phone rang again. The screen said the number was unknown. Max didn't reach for it. Instead, he ran his hand through his hair and his eyes darted back to the window. "Okay, but there's a very good and very reasonable explanation for everything I've done."

"And can you tell me what that explanation is?" she asked.

His eyes turned back to her face. Confusion, doubt, regret and half a dozen other emotions she couldn't identify roiled in his eyes like water about to overflow its banks. She didn't want to leave him and she didn't want him to go. She wanted to step back into the safety of his chest and feel his arm around her. Instead, she took a step back.

"You should go," she said. "I'd leave, but my phone is completely dead and I need to plug it in to charge. I used the final bit of battery life to download three texts from Gerry asking where I was and if his son was okay. I'll call him and sort out with him whether I'm renting a car or if he's going to get someone to pick me up. You've done more than enough. You've been incredible, and I'm always going to be grateful for everything. But having you caught up in my mess isn't good for either of us."

He glanced at his phone again, then back to the window and then finally up to the ceiling. She watched as his eyes closed and his lips moved in what looked like prayer.

"Okay, I'm sorry if I was over the line," he said. He turned back to her, his hand grabbed hers and she didn't pull away. Instead, she stood there, feeling the warmth of his fingers enveloping hers. "I don't want to fight with you and you're right that it isn't my place to grill you about your life. But I'm worried about you and I really do want to help. How about we both take a deep breath and start over? The only sleep I got was the quick nap in the cabin with Fitz on my chest and about thirty minutes on a cot in the back. How about I go into the kitchen, put on a pot of coffee and see about making you some breakfast? You must be starving."

Car tires crunched on the gravel outside. She looked up, her back stiffening in fear. Two shining white cop cars had pulled up outside. Max snatched his phone off the table and texted something so quick it couldn't have been more than four or five letters. The phone beeped back a response almost as quickly.

He frowned and glanced back at the cars. It looked like there was a male officer in one and a female officer in the other, and they appeared to be talking through their open windows.

Max grabbed his leather jacket off the chair and shoved his hands through both sleeves at once, tossing it on with a quick cool flick over his head. "I'm hoping they're just looking for coffee and wondering if the diner's open. Hold on, I'll go talk to them, explain I met the owner and she let me in, which is the actual truth. Just hold on and don't run or anything. Please."

"Okay," she said. "But when you get back, I want you to explain about the owner of this place. I'm only agreeing to coffee on the condition you start answering questions, too."

"Deal." A tired smile crooked his face. It was endearing. "I'll just be a second."

She swung Fitz around to her other hip and watched as Max sauntered down the diner toward the door. There was something about his walk that was somehow both alert and relaxed at the same time, like every move his body made projected both reassurance and protection. Chimes jingled as he pushed through the front door and stepped outside. She looked down. He'd left the keys on the table.

She let out a long breath. Was this some kind of test to see what kind of person she really was and if she wanted to add stolen paramedic vehicle to her rap sheet?

"What's wrong with me?" She looked down at Fitz. He responded with a gurgle and a wide baby-tooth grin. "I barely know Max. He's practically a stranger. I shouldn't care what he thinks of me."

Fitz squealed and waved both hands. She hugged him close. She didn't know what was sadder, the fact that for the past few months the only person she could really talk to was a baby or that she had no idea how much longer he'd even be in her life. She closed her eyes and whispered a desperate prayer, feeling the tears of worry and relief she'd refused to shed in front of Max prick against the corner of her eyes.

Sudden shouts filled the air, panic leaped in her throat and her eyes jerked open. Two uniformed cops were running toward Max, guns drawn. Fear flooded her veins. She knew them. They'd been the two cops who'd shown up at the house weeks ago, who Gerry had accused of trying to blackmail him and whose visit had caused the fighting between Anna and Gerry to intensify. The man with the buzz cut was Officer Bradley and his much shorter partner with the ponytail and baseball cap was Officer Kelly—or at least those seemed to be the names Daisy remembered hearing between Anna and Gerry screaming back and forth at each other.

"Get down!" Officer Bradley shouted, so loudly his voice seemed to shake the window. "Hands up now!"

She had no idea how they'd found her. But whatever their link to all this, they now had Max in their crosshairs. She clutched Fitz to her chest and watched as Max's strong form knelt on the pavement. Fitz whimpered in her arms, as if sensing her fear. She had to get out of there, she had to take Fitz and run, but how could she leave Max in danger?

Oh, Max, I'm so sorry. I dragged you into this.

"Don't shoot! I'm cooperating." Max called loudly. His hands rose. "I demand to see your badges and know what's going on here."

Daisy watched as Officer Kelly's mouth moved but didn't hear the reply through the window. Then Kelly pressed the barrel of her gun into the back of Max's head, while her partner pushed him down into the pavement and cuffed Max's hands behind his back.

"Kelly! Watch him!" Bradley bellowed. "If he moves so much as a muscle, shoot him!"

He started toward the restaurant door. Daisy grabbed Max's keys off the table, slung both bags over her shoulder and ran.

SIX

Frustration filled Max's core as Officer Kelly's weapon pinned him down against the pavement. He'd never once envisioned it was possible for him to feel this much annoyance at seeing cops show up. But these two had broken so many protocols it wasn't funny.

He was sure they were police, though, unlike Smith's lame attempt at pretending to be law enforcement. Their vehicles and uniforms were RCMP and their guns and handcuffs were police issue. Unfortunately, neither of them were the specific detectives he'd been looking forward to seeing.

Faint drizzle began to fall, like the sky still wasn't sure it was ready to rain. Wet pavement pressed against his cheek.

The fact that he'd grown up running around his family's own paintball course and shooting range, with two older brothers, who became cops while he was in grade school, had left Max with a healthy respect for guns and a keen sense of how to get away from them when he needed to. But he had Daisy to think about, Trent and Chloe were on their way and it was probably in his best interest to not risk getting arrested or shot.

Besides, these two gung ho cops probably thought he'd helped kidnap a baby.

"I'm not resisting arrest," he said, hoping the words would calm Kelly down. He wondered if Kelly was a first name or last name. But that was a far less important question than why they were here, how they'd known how to find them and whether these were two of the cops his brother warned him about.

"My name is Max Henry," he said, as loudly and clearly as he could. "I'm a paramedic. Feel free to check my wallet."

"You were told to keep your mouth shut," she said. He felt her weight shift and then he felt her pat down his pockets, including reaching around for the breast one he never used. She took his phone as well as his wallet. He wondered if he'd had his keys on him if she'd have taken them, too.

"Look, I know why you're here and I know what you're after," he said quickly. "But she's a really good person. She has a good heart, she loves that baby and I'm convinced she didn't kidnap him."

As he heard himself saying the words, he felt the certainty of them growing stronger. Yes, he believed in Daisy. Despite everything the mysterious Jane had said on the phone and despite Daisy's defensive admission that she had a troubled past. There was just something stubborn that beat inside him even louder than his doubt. Maybe it was hope. Maybe it was faith. But whatever it was, it kept coming back to the look of love that had burned in Daisy's eyes as she'd surrendered to an armed killer to help save Fitz.

He also had no doubt that the moment she'd seen the cops converge and pin him down, she'd run for his vehicle, yanked the camouflaged cover off and taken Fitz to safety.

Lord, please be with Daisy and Fitz now. Keep them safe. Get them the help they need.

"Bradley!" Officer Kelly shouted. "Get out here! Quick! He's got sugar maple money!"

He had what? Max had no idea what that was and only had about twenty bucks in his wallet. But whatever it was she'd found, it made Officer Bradley practically barge through the door and pelt down the steps.

"What?" he shouted. "You sure?"

"Pretty sure!" Officer Kelly giggled and while he couldn't prove it, Max suspected she was waving something around. Officer Bradley chortled, too. It was a loud and greedy sound. "He has a badge, though," Kelly added. "He's a paramedic."

Bradley's laughter stopped cold. "You really sure he's not a cop?"

"No, just a paramedic, rapid response and air ambulance. I've checked his ID."

Max was yanked to his feet and half dragged, half propelled himself across the pavement toward the closest cop car. He'd never had any reason to distrust a cop before, let alone fear one. Police had been his heroes for as long as he remembered. He'd been barely ten when his oldest brother, Jacob, entered the police academy and then twelve when Trent followed in his footsteps. Now they were his partners and his allies in saving lives.

Yet as Officer Bradley threw him against the car, every vague story he'd heard either of his brothers tell about how bad people existed in every walk of life suddenly clattered inside him. Injustice stung harder than the feeling of his body hitting the hood.

The drizzle turned a light sprinkling of rain

that ran down the back of his neck and seemed to seep into his skin. He had to keep his cool. Trent and Chloe would be there soon enough. He just had to chill until then.

Officer Bradley eased his grip slightly and Max took the opportunity to spin around so quickly that the cop didn't realize what was happening until Max was staring him straight in the eye. "Officers, again, I demand to see your badges and to know what I'm being charged with."

Officer Bradley spluttered. He was an unremarkable-looking man, Max thought, maybe a few years older than Max was, with a square jaw, short buzzed hair and a stance that reminded him of hundreds of officers that he'd met at hundreds of accident and crime scenes across Ontario. He scanned the man's uniform. Bradley and Kelly had covered their badge numbers with electrical tape. Classy.

"Cool your jets, doc," Bradley said. A smile he probably thought looked real crossed his face. "Nobody needs to get arrested today. We just want to ask you some questions. Cooperate fully and we'll let you go."

Riiiiiiiiiight.

"Questions about what?" Max asked, with a blank look as genuine as Bradley's smile.

Although, he didn't need to ask. He already knew the answer would be some combination of Daisy, Fitz, the death of Anna and whatever crime Gerry had committed that had Trent and Chloe speeding toward him.

"The money, idiot!" Officer Kelly waved two golden Canadian hundred-dollar bills in his face. "Where did you get this?"

He had no idea. He'd been sure the only cash he had was the twenty in his wallet and some change in the console of his truck. Unless Daisy had refused to take no for an answer when she'd offered to cover the cost of repairs, and so she had slipped it in his jacket. He wouldn't put it past her. But it was equally possible he'd stuffed it in his pocket months ago and forgotten.

"What? Why?" Max spluttered and barely caught himself from outright laughing. "You took my phone, took my wallet and handcuffed me all over two hundred bucks? I honestly have no idea how long that's been in my jacket."

Officer Kelly looked at her partner. He sneered.

"You think we're idiots?" He leaned in closer. "This is sugar maple money."

He said the three words like the mere sound of them was explosive.

"If you say so," Max said, "but I have no idea what that means. Honestly."

A truck shimmered on the horizon and Max held his breath as it slowed. Then it sped up and kept going. It wasn't Trent and it wasn't help.

"Look, we're not playing!" Bradley's eyes bulged. His hand balled into a fist that hovered in the air, threatening to fly. "Don't get smart with us. We found you with sugar maple money in your pocket. That's a federal crime!"

Max almost laughed. Why? How? The officer had to be bluffing. Trent's warning that Daisy was a potential witness in a major organized-crime case flickered through the back of Max's mind. But would Daisy really have blithely stuffed evidence from a federal crime in his pocket?

"You can't be serious." Max flinched his aching shoulders in an involuntary shrug before realizing his hands were cuffed behind his back. He couldn't believe a word either of these two were saying. Their amateur attempts to shake him down would have been laughable were it not for the very real damage he suspected Bradley was more than happy to cause.

How long could he stand there, stalling and buying time until Trent and Chloe got there?

With every moment that passed, Daisy and Fitz were probably getting farther and farther away. "I've heard of maple sugar, maple syrup, maple trees and the red maple leaf in the middle of the Canadian flag. But I have no clue why you're waving two hundred bucks in my face like they're some kind of golden tickets."

Officer Bradley's fist flinched. Max's jaw didn't.

"Bradley! Stop. Let me," Kelly yelled. She stepped in between them. Okay, so it was clear who was the good cop. "Look, Mister..."

"Henry," he supplied. "Max Henry. I know my ID says Maxwell, but the only person who calls me that now is my mother. Although back in school, the jerks at school used to sing that stupid song about Maxwell with the silver hammer at me. I don't think they realized it was about a serial killer."

Kelly's smile grew tight.

"Well, Max," she said. "We're part of a special police task force investigating counterfeit currency. It's a huge investigation involving very special computer programs and equipment, and it's our job to find out who's making that fake money and take them out. Last we heard, only a small batch of prototype bills had even been made, and somehow two of them ended up in your wallet."

Max felt his jaw drop. He wasn't faking it.

"We got an anonymous call from someone giving us your description and letting us know where to find you. So clearly, someone out there is not your friend." Kelly's artificial smile grew sweeter. Max wondered if the helpful tipster's name was Jane.

The cop continued, "Now, we're really not interested in some low-level guy running around with two hundred dollars in his wallet. We want the big fish who have the design skills, technology and equipment to print millions of these. So here's what's going to happen. You're going to tell us exactly where you got this money from and where we can find that person, and we'll go bother them instead and pretend we never met you. This doesn't need to get unpleasant."

Her voice trailed off, leaving an ominous note of threat in its wake.

"Yeah, I got it," Max said and he did. He got it perfectly clearly, despite the fact he suspected a whole bunch of lies were mixed up in the truth of what they were saying. "I honestly had no idea that money was fake and couldn't tell you where it came from."

Bradley swore under his breath. "This guy's wasting our time. Let's take him for a little drive and see if that jogs his memory."

Two large hands grabbed Max, yanked him sideways and forced him around the car. Warning bells blared in the back of his mind. This whole situation had gone from almost funny to downright serious in a heartbeat. He was no use to anyone if he was held hostage by two corrupt cops.

"Look, I didn't want to do this, but my brother is Detective Trent Henry with RCMP Vice," Max said. "He's on his way here to meet me. He'll be here any minute."

The words hit the air like a thunderclap. Instantly, Bradley's hands dropped from Max's body and his face went a sickly shade. Kelly gasped, a simple sound filled with fear and shock that made it clear she knew exactly who Max's older brother was.

Suddenly, Max remembered what it was like to be a nerdy preteen with the kind of quick mouth that had landed him on the wrong end of those school-yard bullies' fists. It had taken a broken arm before Trent and Jacob had sat him down and told him firmly that sometimes there was no shame in letting the dangerous people of the world know who his family was.

Henry brothers came out swinging for each other. They protected each other, and right now, that protection included Fitz and Daisy.

Curses flew from Bradley's lips like bullets. Then he turned to Kelly. "We have no choice. I'm sorry. We can't have him talking. We're going to have to kill him."

Raindrops splattered against the windshield. The rapid-response unit's engine purred silently beneath Daisy. Fitz whimpered in the back seat, with that little cough-like whine in the back of his throat that indicated he was thinking of crying.

"Hush," Daisy whispered. Her hand slid back between the two front seats, gave his shoulder a tender squeeze and nudged a teething ring back into his mouth. Then her gaze snapped back to the scene unfolding on the dashboard camera.

Max had hidden his vehicle so well, she could barely see the scene unfolding in the parking lot until she'd turned the vehicle on, and the dashboard camera had sprung to life. From there, it was just a matter of angling and focus. While the microphone barely picked up their voices, she could see and hear enough to know he was in trouble.

She prayed. She had to take Fitz to safety. But she couldn't just leave Max while there remained even a possibility that he could escape and run to her. The thought of him pelting toward the vehicle only to discover she'd stolen it was unthinkable, no matter what he might think of her or what he thought she'd done. So she'd waited and watched while they'd pinned him, cuffed him and thrown him against the car, blaming herself and feeling a painful ache grow in her heart.

Why hadn't they let him go yet? Surely, once he explained the situation and told them everything, they'd realize none of her crimes were his fault. He'd wanted her to go to police and now here were two police he could send chasing after her. All he had to do was point them in her direction.

But for whatever reason, instead it seemed the two officers were arguing loudly while Max stood between them with his limbs tensed, like he was waiting for his moment to move. Snatches of their voices filtered through the speaker like she was just catching the last word or two of every sentence: *can't...money... detective...kill him.*

But still, something inside her argued stubbornly that no matter how it looked, Max was okay, that the cops would realize their mistake and take those handcuffs off at any moment now and that she was in more danger sticking around to watch than he was.

And yet, she didn't move.

Her cell phone buzzed back to life in the dashboard holster charger where she'd plugged it in. She glanced down. There were six new messages from Gerry. It sounded like he was spiraling.

Daisy! It's Gerald Pearce. Please text me back.

Where are you? Where's Fitz?

I had some police officers come to meet you at the safe house and you weren't there.

TEXT ME. NOW.

I'm sorry if my last text was harsh.

Just text me. Please. I'm not angry. Just worried.
Please, I just want to know my son's still alive.

Guilt stabbed her heart. A small voice in the back of her mind reminded her that Max was convinced that Gerry was some kind of criminal mastermind. But having marital and relationship problems didn't make him a killer, and he'd always seemed more confused and volatile than anything else. He was still her boss and Fitz's father, and had the right to know his baby was alive.

She grabbed her phone and texted back a quick and vague message, telling him that Fitz was doing just fine, she was still near Algonquin Provincial Park, that she'd stopped to sleep for the night and that she'd be on her way again soon. Then her eyes closed and she let her agony turn to prayer.

What would happen if she just walked into a police station with Fitz and told them the whole story? Would she really be arrested? Would she put Fitz in danger?

The sound of ringing filled the cab. The call display told her it was Gerry's office number at Pearce Enterprises. She pulled the phone from the holder, took a deep breath and hit the red button to answer. "Hello?"

Rhythmic crackling sounded down the line, like the static from a bad connection or the turning of an old-fashioned music box key.

"Hello?" she said again, louder. "Gerry! Can you hear me?"

No answer. Had he somehow dialed by accident or was the connection so bad he couldn't hear her? She glanced back to the camera. Whatever the officers had been arguing about, they were done talking. Kelly popped the trunk of the car. Bradley waved his gun at Max, gesturing him toward it.

Fear brushed her spine. Okay, now what was this?

"Look, Gerry, I can't hear you and I've got to go," she said. "I'll call you back as soon as I can."

But the sound of music playing made her freeze with the phone to her ear. It was a lullaby, high-pitched and tinkling, and she recognized it in an instant. It was the sound of the music box in Fitz's room. It was one Daisy had played him every night to put him to sleep.

"Who is this?" she snapped. "What do you want?"

"I want that baby." The voice was female and distorted. "He belongs to me, and you will give him to me."

"He belongs with his father." The phone shook in Daisy's hand. "Whoever you are, you're not his mother. His mother was Jane, and Jane is dead."

The voice laughed, a loud, large cackle that transitioned into a terrifying scream.

Daisy's shaking fingers stabbed at the disconnect button, missing twice until she finally hit it. The phone fell silent. Sudden tears rushed her eyes as her heart pounded too fast to even begin to process what she'd just heard.

Then she gripped the steering wheel. No, she wasn't going to sit around on the side of the road, in someone else's vehicle and let someone taunt her into falling apart with creepy music. She was going to get Fitz to safety. Somehow. Somewhere. But she'd figure it out and Fitz would be okay, because right now his tiny life was in her hands and that was all that mattered.

A gun blast yanked her attention back to the camera. Max was running down the side of the road, dodging trees and rocks. Daisy dropped the phone and grabbed the keys. Time to move.

"Hang on, it might get bumpy," she said. She got out and yanked the camouflage cover off the vehicle, then she leaped back in, whispered a prayer and put the car into Drive.

Officer Kelly ran back to her car and Bradley ran after Max. But Max was running toward her hiding spot, growing closer to her and Fitz with every step, with hope shining like fire in his eyes that his vehicle might still be there.

"Come on, Max. Please don't stop. Just keep running. I'm here. All you've got to do is make it here, leap in and then we'll go."

A loud crackling sound split the air. Max hollered and stumbled forward.

A cry escaped Daisy's lips even as her eyes struggled to make sense of what she was seeing. Then she saw the black device in Bradley's hand and the long wire attached to the dart sticking out of Max's back.

He'd been hit with a long-range Taser dart.

SEVEN

Max tried to push himself to his feet but his legs gave way. He lay there on the pavement, panting and helpless, as his mind struggled for a second to process the crackling sound that rang in his ears and the sharp pinch in his back. Desperately he spun around, dislodging the wire from his back, and only then realized what had happened.

He'd been hit by a Taser.

Bradley stopped, still a few feet away, put the Taser away and reached for his gun. The roar of an engine filled the air.

Max struggled to his hands and knees. Thankfully Bradley had shot it from a distance and had only got one dart in him. Otherwise, he wouldn't even be able to move. He tried to push himself back to his feet.

"Stay down!" Bradley ordered. "Don't move!"

"I'm down!" Max crouched low and raised

his hands above his head. "I surrender! Okay! I surrender!"

He had no other choice. That was it. It was over.

Clearly they'd wanted him alive, though he wasn't sure how reassuring that was.

The sound of the vehicle grew closer. Headlights glared against the gray sky, their refracted light shining off the drizzling rain. It was flying straight at them.

Bradley shouted and leaped back. Max dropped to the ground and tried to roll out of his path. But then the vehicle swerved, spinning in an arc between him and the officer, and screeched to a stop. He looked up. The familiar white side of his rapid-response unit was a foot from his face. The passenger door flew open.

Daisy leaned toward him, her blond hair tumbled around her shoulders and determination blazed in her eyes. She reached for him. "Come on. Get in!"

He forced his wobbly legs to spring and threw himself toward her and into the safety of the vehicle. Her hand grabbed his shoulder and helped pull him up. He tumbled onto the passenger seat.

"You came back for me," he said. "I can't believe you're really here."

She didn't meet his gaze but the faint blush that rose to her cheekbones said that she'd heard him. He twisted around and struggled for his seat belt, his hands still cuffed behind his back. She leaned over, yanked it over his chest and buckled it in. The scent of her filled his senses, her dark eyes met his and something jolted inside him like residual electricity.

"Don't worry," she said, "I'll get those off you as soon as we're stopped somewhere safe."

Gunfire sounded behind them. Max heard the clang of a bullet hitting the back of his vehicle.

"Hang on!" Daisy sat up straight, yanked the gearshift into Reverse and hit the accelerator. The truck shot backward. She tapped the breaks, shifted again and the vehicle spun forward. The passenger door beside him slammed from the impact. The vehicle righted, she hit the gas again and they shot down the road. Her eyes glanced to the rearview mirror. "Officer Kelly's in her car and coming after us. Officer Bradley is still running back to his car."

His head swam. "You know them?"

"They came by the house a few months ago," she said. "Gerry said they'd tried to blackmail him. They're the reason he said some cops weren't to be trusted."

He had a hunch that was as close to a told-you-so as he was ever going to get. Sirens sounded through the air behind them. Lights flashed. Her eyes cut to the rearview mirror.

"You do want me to outrun them, right?" she asked. Worry lines creased the delicate skin around her eyes. "Because if you've got another idea, you'd better tell me now."

He could still only hear one siren, but it would be joined by a second one soon enough when Bradley got back to his car. The hope of meeting up with Trent and Chloe anytime soon was fading in the distance.

"Officer Kelly wanted to take me somewhere and question me illegally," he said. "Officer Bradley wanted to kill me. The only thing they could really agree on is they wanted me to ride in the trunk. I still believe we've got to talk to the cops, but those two sure aren't the ones we need to talk to."

"Okay," she said. Her jaw set. "Then hold on and trust me."

She reached back between the seats for Fitz, as if feeling for the warmth of his skin. Then both hands grabbed the wheel again. Rocks and trees flew past.

Max watched as she inched the speedometer upward. The road narrowed, with steep ditches on either side. She inched closer to the gravel verge, holding the vehicle steady with a control and calm that almost stunned him even more than the Taser had. Kelly's police car loomed large in the rearview mirror.

He had to trust Daisy knew what she was doing. He had to believe she wouldn't do anything reckless with Fitz in the car, even with a potential killer on their tail.

Then he saw the narrow metal bridge, no more than a car's width, leading through the woods to their right. Daisy yanked the steering wheel hard to the right, popping the vehicle in and out of Neutral, before throwing the emergency break on and off again. The vehicle drifted, spinning around in a circle as it careened toward the trees. Kelly's cop car flew past so close it almost clipped them.

Prayer surged through him. Then he felt the rough rumble of the metal access bridge under their tires and the vehicle shuddered safely to a stop. Max looked up. Thick trees pressed them in on every side. A tiny road lay beneath them. She'd slid them over the narrow access bridge as precisely and narrowly as threading a needle.

His heart pounded. "I thought you'd lost your license."

"For speeding, years ago, and I got it back." She flushed and a dazzling smile flashed across her face. She undid her belt, turned around and checked the back seat. Then she laughed. "Fitz is asleep again. Let's hope he naps for a while this time."

She reached to put the car into Drive. But before they could move, a screech of tires filled the air, then a loud bang and the horrifying scream of metal scraping against rock.

They were sounds he'd heard a hundred times in his nightmares. Sounds that meant someone had been in a terrible accident and that somebody could die if he didn't save them.

"Let me out!" Max said. "Please!"

She leaned over him and pulled back the door handle. Max leaped out. Daisy looked back, but all she could see were trees. That was the point. She'd maneuvered them specifically so that they'd be hidden from the road and now he was running back toward it.

Max disappeared down the path for a few seconds, then he was back. "Officer Kelly tried to turn back to follow us, lost control and crashed into the ditch. I have to call the accident in and go make sure she's okay."

"You can't be serious!" Daisy pushed the

driver's-side door open. "Call it in, sure, but don't go back. She just tried to take you hostage! Her partner wants to kill you!"

A siren roared closer. It passed. Then it disappeared in the distance. Guess that meant Officer Bradley wasn't stopping to check on his partner.

"I told you when we met," he said. "I have a duty to do whatever I can to save a life, unless doing so puts that person or someone else in danger."

"Does that include putting yourself in danger?" she shot back.

His shoulders flinched like he was trying to throw his hands in the air and had forgotten he was still in handcuffs. Didn't he get how ridiculous this was? He was actually planning on running toward an accident with his hands behind his back.

"Yup," he said. "I go assess the scene and determine if helping the wounded puts myself, them or someone else in danger. If it poses a threat, I just call it in and back off. But right now, we have an accident victim in a ditch on a rural highway road. Even when I call it in, I don't know how long it will take anyone else to reach her. She could bleed out. She could have a heart attack. Any number of things could happen, and I won't know until I go check!"

He stood there, staring at her, a long breath spreading out between them and the faint, persistent drizzle running down the lines of his face. Then she turned the engine off and leaped out.

"Fine," she said. "I'm going with you, because you're going to need a working pair of hands and maybe we'll be able to grab a pair of handcuff keys. But you've got five minutes. That's it. Hopefully that will be long enough for you to do whatever assessing you need to do."

He didn't argue. He just grinned and then ran toward the accident. "Grab the jump bag!"

Fitz was still asleep. Daisy pulled the cover over his car seat and unclipped it from the car seat base. She picked the car seat up with one hand, grabbed the red bag with the other and ran after Max. The road was clear. The police car lay ahead, a white hunk of metal, nose down in the three-foot ditch. Then she saw Kelly slumped against the steering wheel, her dark hair falling over her neck and the airbag covering her face. Max jumped into the ditch.

Daisy climbed down after him. She set Fitz by her feet. "Tell me what we do."

"ABC," he called. "Airways, then breathing and then circulation. Our first problem is that the airbag should've deflated after impact. But looks like it malfunctioned and she's got tangled up in it. Do you still have your scissors?"

"Yeah." She yanked them from her belt.

"Great," he said. "Open the door and then pop the airbag. Get it away from her face. I think it's blocking her nose and mouth."

She did so, watching the airbag hiss and deflate like a pale gray balloon. The officer's eyes were closed. Max leaned in and put his face close to Kelly's, then Daisy heard him breathe a prayer of thanks.

"She's breathing," he said, "though I'm not sure how long she would've been if you hadn't cleared her airways. The airbag could've suffocated her. No visible contusions or lacerations, so bleeding out isn't likely."

"But she's unconscious," Daisy said.

"Open the second flap of the jump bag, and you should find a vial. It's smelling salts. Open it and wave it under her nose."

"Why would you possibly wake her up?"

"It's my duty as a paramedic," he said. "I have to try to wake her up, or I stay with her until she regains consciousness. I can't leave an unconcious woman at the side of the road, even if her partner did just threaten to kill me."

Now was no time to argue. She reached into the bag and found them exactly where he'd told her. She yanked the cap back. A pungent smell of ammonia that put the stench in the cabin to shame filled her airways. She held her breath and stuck the vial under Kelly's nose.

The woman's eyes shot open and her head jerked back. She glanced at Daisy.

"Get away from me!" She swore and rummaged around as if searching for her gun. They weren't going to give her time to find it.

"Time to go!" Max said.

Agreed. Daisy capped the smelling salts, dropped them in the bag and scooped up the car seat. They scrambled back up the slope. A few paces later and they all were back in his vehicle, with Fitz still asleep. She turned the engine over and glanced at the dash. The whole thing had taken no more than six minutes. Max slid onto the passenger seat, and she helped him close the door and buckle his seat belt again. "Sorry, we didn't grab the handcuff key."

"No worries," he said. "Now, follow my instructions exactly and I'll talk you through how to call it in on the computer. It'll take less than thirty seconds, I promise." She hit the buttons he told her to and logged the GPS coordinates and an emergency code. Then she gunned the engine. They shot down the narrow track, deeper into the forest. A gunshot echoed behind them, far in the distance.

Max leaned back against the seat.

"Emergency crews will reach her soon," he said. "Investigators will also make sure the vehicle manufacturer knows about the airbag malfunction, in case it's part of a larger problem and they have to do a recall. You do realize something that simple could've killed her. You might have saved her life."

They pushed through the trees. She couldn't imagine what it was like to be him, always running into danger and saving lives. Stones bumped beneath their sturdy wheels. Branches scraped the windows. "What do they know about Fitz?"

"They weren't looking for Fitz," he said. "They were looking for something called sugar maple money."

She could feel him watching her face carefully as if gauging her response.

She shrugged. "Smith and Jones mentioned that, too. I'm guessing that's a Canadian thing?"

"Not a Canadian thing I've ever heard of," he said. "What did Smith and Jones say about it?"

"I found some money in Gerry's car," she said. "They were all hundred-dollar bills. I scattered them in the cabin when we ran, because I knew that would slow them down. They called it sugar maple money."

"You slipped two bills into the pocket of my jacket."

Heat rose to her cheeks. "I told you I'd help pay for repairs and the car seat."

"And I told you not to bother."

Another dirt track appeared to their right and she darted down it. A small signpost for the provincial park flew past as a blink in the headlights. She waited for him to explain further, but he didn't. Trees crowded the path. Jagged rocks jutted around them. Then a lake spread out, silent and gray beside them. She pulled to a stop.

"I could be wrong, but I think we've lost them," she said.

"I think so, too," he said. Towering rocks and trees hemmed them in on all sides. She cut the engine and silence fell, punctuated only by the sound of the rain pattering on the trees, the water lapping gently against the shore and their own ragged breaths.

"Are you going to tell me what's so special about sugar maple money?" she asked.

"It's counterfeit," he said. She gasped. But he didn't meet her eye. Instead, he looked straight ahead through the windshield. "It's a very good-quality counterfeit—very hard to do and involving a very complex operation. I'm sorry, Daisy, but I think it's time you accept you may have been working for a crime lord."

EIGHT

He'd tried to tell her earlier. He'd tried to ease her into realizing that Gerry was a criminal back at the diner, to help her see why she should cooperate with Trent and Chloe's investigation, even if they ended up arresting her.

But he could tell in a glance that she still didn't believe it.

"What we need to worry about right now is getting your handcuffs off," she said. Daisy undid her seat belt, then she reached over and undid his. Her hair brushed softly against the scruff of his day-old shadow.

The scent of her filled his senses. She was so close that all he'd have to do was bend his head and his lips would brush hers. Jane's voice echoed in his mind, asking him just how well he thought he knew her. "Now, if you want to turn your back to me, I'll see if I can open them."

He shifted around in his seat. "They're metal, not plastic zip ties. We'll need a key."

"Don't worry, I might be able to do something." Her fingers ran along the edges of the handcuffs and brushed over his skin. "I just need something from your jump bag."

"Help yourself," he said, though he wasn't sure what she was going to find in there.

She rummaged around and came up with a long, thin safety pin. She bent it. "Now, hold your hands as straight as you can."

He did as she asked. Scattered raindrops fell, splattering the windows in thick drops. He felt her slender fingers of one hand hold his hands together, as the other slowly and carefully worked the pin into the handcuff lock like a key. "How did you learn to do that?"

"My stepfather is a retired police constable," she said. "He started living with my mother and me when I was about nine or ten. He taught me a few things."

"Is he why you don't trust cops?"

The gentle movement of her fingers against his skin stopped again. He looked up into the passenger window and saw her reflection there, looking back at him from the tinted glass. Her reflected eyes held his gaze for a long moment. Then she turned back to the handcuffs.

"He's why I don't trust people," she said. "He's a horrible man, but he was charming at first. Something changed after my half sister was born. He was rough with my mother. He was tough on me. I'm not sure how or why he lost his job, but suddenly he was home every day, drinking and gambling on whatever he could bet money on. I was eleven."

Something metallic clicked. He felt her fingers run along the inside of the handcuffs, brushing against the insides of his wrists. The cuffs didn't move. She sighed.

"Please keep going," he said. "I like listening. I think it keeps me from fidgeting."

He watched as raindrops fell heavier against the window, running in long lines down the reflection of her face. She went back to working on the lock.

"My mother and stepfather had four kids," she said, "one right after the other—Gilly, Candi, Michelle and Albert—three girls and a boy. He hit me for the first time after Gilly was born. Not a real hit, he'd say, just a slap across the face because I wanted to go out to a youth club and he wanted me to stay home, so he could drink. His slap was so hard my teeth rattled. I called the cops for the first time when I was fourteen, but I guess he had enough friends on the force who believed him when he said I was dramatic. When I was sixteen, it got so bad I went to live with my aunt."

He heard another click and then he felt the handcuffs slide off his right wrist. He held his breath and fought the urge to move.

"I graduated early and hitchhiked around Scotland, Ireland and Wales. I hiked around some of Europe, too, took odd jobs and saved my money. It was glorious actually. I loved the freedom. But then social services threatened to put my half siblings in care unless my mother took better care of them, and my aunt couldn't afford to support them all on her own. So I went home and told my stepfather I'd pay off what he owed the landlord in exchange for his car. He agreed. Then he called the cops on me, claiming I'd stolen both his car and some other stuff that was actually mine."

His other hand fell free. The urge to turn around and face her filled his core. Instead, he reached back, grabbed both her hands and held her fingers tight. She hesitated, then looped her fingers through his. His eyes met hers again in the rain-smeared glass.

"What happened?" he asked.

"My mother begged me to plead guilty in exchange for probation. Told me if I did, they'd let me move back home and everything would be different. Every instinct in my body screamed that it was the wrong decision. But I trusted her over my instincts because I was nineteen and foolish. My stepfather kicked me out again the next day."

"You weren't foolish," he said. "You were a good person, with a good heart, who was trying to do the right thing and someone took advantage of that."

Then he took a deep breath and prayed his words would come out right.

"Just like I worry they're doing now," he added.

"Because you think Fitz's father is a crime lord."

She pulled her fingers out of his. He turned around. His hands reached for hers again. She didn't let him take them.

"It's the only thing that could possibly make sense of everything that's happened," he said. "Gerry told you not to trust the cops. You find counterfeit money in his car. Both of his wives are dead."

"Well, maybe I'm not ready to believe that means he's a criminal yet." Her voice rose. "Maybe I want to hold on to the hope that there's another answer and that Fitz is going to have a better life ahead of him than one parent who's dead and another who's in prison. Maybe, it's because I actually know Gerald Pearce. He's exactly what you think an absentminded inventor would be like. He's distracted. He's forgetful and confused. He's emotionally erratic and volatile. Those are his symptoms. Sounds like early-onset dementia, right?"

"Possibly," he said, carefully. "Or it could be a mental illness like depression, considering his wife died less than a year ago and he rushed into a new marriage. Or it could be a head trauma, postconcussive syndrome, some kind of poison or nervous system disorder, especially if combined with shakes. It could be any number of things. You can't look at three symptoms and jump to a diagnosis."

"But you can look at two or three facts and conclude someone's a criminal?" she asked.

It wasn't the same thing. He closed his eyes and prayed. If he told Daisy about Trent and Chloe, she'd be livid and he'd have done exactly what Trent told him not to do. But surely Trent's motivation was that he didn't want her to either spike the investigation or take off running, and she couldn't exactly do either in the woods. But she could get even more upset. He opened his mouth, but she jumped in before he could say anything.

"Gerry works five days a week and was always away at one of his companies," she said. "But he comes home on the weekends, and when he does, he always makes a beeline for Fitz and brings him some ridiculous new toy. I don't believe he has the mental wherewithal to run a criminal enterprise. I never believed he was evil and calculating. I believe he's romantically foolish, not particularly methodical and he loves his son. Maybe I'm wrong about everything. But my whole life, my instincts where the only thing that kept me alive. Whenever I didn't listen to them, I paid the price, and right now, my gut is all I've got."

Her eyes met his. Tears shone like gold in their depths. She held his gaze for one long, agonizing moment and everything inside him wanted to pull her into his arms and hold her. Instead, she turned and pushed through the door and stepped out into the drizzling rain.

For a moment, he thought she was going to take off running. But then she stopped just a couple of feet away from the vehicle, with her back to him and her face to the lake. He watched as she wrapped her arms around herself.

She's wrong. Her instincts aren't all she has. She has me.

Lord, what do I do? How do I help her?

His hand reached for the door handle, but his eyes glanced at the phone she'd left mounted in the charger on the dashboard. He picked it up, typed the special secure number he knew would be redirected to his brother's phone. Now all he had to do was compose a message that anyone intercepting wouldn't understand.

It's 'swell. Not secure. All safe.

He watched the message go and prayed that his pitiful attempt at a coded message would get through. *It's (Max)'swell. (Phone line) not secure. (But we are) all safe.* A minute passed slowly. Then a second. Then finally the phone beeped. A new message had come in from an unknown number, but he had no doubt who it was.

Cute. Glad to hear it. Picked up what you left in the ditch. Stay off the grid.

Daisy didn't know why she was crying. It was like all sorts of tears—fear, frustration, sadness and relief—had been building inside her for hours and now they were all rushing out so quickly she could barely breathe.

Anna was dead. The house was gone. Smith and Jones had tried to kill her. Two corrupt cops had threatened Max. The money from Gerry's car was counterfeit.

Help me, God. I feel like I'm drowning. It's all too much. It's more than I can take.

Cold rain poured down her body and soaked her skin. The urge to run pounded deep inside her chest, but something invisible and unbreakable tethered her to the tiny child sleeping in the vehicle. A door slammed behind her. Then she heard footsteps crossing the muddy ground.

"All I care about is keeping Fitz safe," she said. She didn't turn and wasn't even sure he could hear her. "But I don't know how."

"I know," Max said.

The sound of his footsteps stopped. She heard the rustle of waterproof fabric and then he draped an emergency blanket around her head and shoulders. She wiped the tears from her eyes and blinked hard to keep any more from falling.

"Jane phoned me," she said, "after those cops showed up at the diner. I forgot to tell you, what with everything else going on. She called from the general Pearce company number, demanded I give her Fitz and said he belonged with her. What if she's really Jane? What if Jane isn't dead? What if the police dig up her coffin and discover there's someone else buried there in the cemetery?" A sob filled her throat. She gasped a breath. "She tried to scare me. She tried to upset me. She laughed and screamed and played the music from Fitz's favorite music box over the phone."

"Clearly she has no idea how strong you really are." Max's voice was warm and deep in her ear. She didn't turn but instead stepped back toward him. He parted his arms to make room for her, his hands brushed lightly against her arms and she leaned back against his chest, letting his warmth fill her body.

She shook her head. "I don't feel strong. I feel like a fool."

"But you are strong," he said, "and incredibly brave. You might feel like a fool, but you're really not. You're compassionate. You're quick thinking. You're brilliant, Daisy. You're the most amazing person I've ever met."

His hands ran down her arms, she slid her hands up to meet them, and their fingers linked together. She couldn't remember the last time anyone gave her a compliment, let alone several of them in a row. "You're pretty great, too, and I'm sorry I dragged you into this mess."

"You didn't drag me into anything." He pulled her closer. "I chose to get involved. I chose to help you and Fitz and to make your problems my problem. Just like you chose to come back for me."

But why? She let go of his hands and turned to face him. Her eyes searched his. Questions filled her mind, but she didn't have the courage to let them pass her lips. Why was he standing by her when he had every reason to leave? Why had he rescued Fitz and brought him back to her? And why had she found it so impossible to just drive away and leave him?

The dark centers of his green eyes deepened. He wrapped his arms around her waist, she slid her hands around his neck and he pulled her closer still. Something unfamiliar fluttered in her chest. She'd never craved the feeling of being held in a man's arms before. Watching the train wreck that her mother's marriage had been and hearing how Gerry and Anna squabbled had cured her from ever wanting any man for herself.

But now here she was, burying her head in the crook of his neck and clinging to him, as if he was the only strong and solid thing keeping her tethered. He held her just as tightly, and for a single terrifying moment, everything felt right and safe inside her chest, in a way it never had before.

Then she felt the breath of him on her face. The stubble of his jaw brushed against her skin and she tilted her face up toward him. Their lips softly touched.

Fitz coughed from the back seat, then he whimpered with that little warning half cry that meant he was about to start howling.

"It's okay, Fitz. I'm here! I'm coming!" She pulled out of Max's arms and stumbled back across the muddy ground to the vehicle. What was she thinking? Standing out here in the trees and the drizzling rain, with her lips barely touching Max's, just a breath away from letting him sweep her into his chest and deepen their kiss.

"Why don't I drive?" Max suggested. "He'll probably be hungry again in an hour or so, and by then hopefully we'll be somewhere we can feed and change him."

He slid his hand over his jaw, like he was wiping away the memory of the fleeting kiss. She nodded. "Thank you."

They got back in his vehicle and he started driving. The wheels crunched over rocks and dirt. Tree branches brushed against the window. She pushed a teething cookie into Fitz's hands and heard his cries turn to those gurgles of delight that always filled her heart with joy. Light rain splattered on the windshield and the roof. Her eyes closed.

Thank You, God, for Max. Thank You that he's here. Thank You that I'm not alone.

She didn't expect to sleep and didn't even notice when she started drifting. All she knew was that her eyes were heavy and staying closed.

After a while, the engine picked up speed as the road turned from rough to smooth under their tires. The sound of the rain grew heavier on the roof. She heard the faint sounds of Fitz gurgling again and Max switching on the radio and searching for a channel. Then music filled the cab. Old hymns she knew from childhood and new songs she'd never heard rose and fell, mingling ancient words and modern instruments.

Max started to sing along. His voice was rich and deep, slightly off pitch and a bit hit-and-miss with the tune. It wasn't the kind of voice anyone would choose for the choir or put on the radio. But there was something comforting and endearing about it. Adorable even.

Eventually, the vehicle slowed to a gentle stop. She heard the door open and close, and Fitz's cheerful chatter, but even then she didn't fully wake up until she heard footsteps crunching on the gravel.

She opened her eyes. Unfamiliar farmland filled her vision.

"Where are we? Why did we stop?" She sat up and glanced over. The driver's seat was empty. But her heart didn't fully begin to race until her hand reached back instinctively for Fitz's car seat and found the back seat empty, too.

Max and Fitz were gone.

NINE

Max slid the car seat higher up on his arm and walked up the winding path to the Henry family farmhouse. The sun sat high in the sky, peeking its way through the shifting tableau of clouds. Fitz chattered softly beside him.

Guilt dripped down somewhere inside him and pooled in his chest. He felt bad for leaving Daisy napping in the car, even if only for a few minutes. But the opportunity to grab even just five minutes to talk to his parents and fill them in on everything that happened before he introduced them to Daisy had seemed too important to pass up.

Besides, she'd seemed to be sleeping so peacefully, and considering what she'd been through, he knew she needed the rest. She'd barely stirred when Fitz had started fussing for a diaper change the moment the van had stopped. Fatigue was a health hazard after all, he told himself, bad for the body and bad for the mind. It had just passed noon and by his guess, she'd barely had three hours of sleep since yesterday. Not that he'd had much more.

They were both overtired, lacking sleep and running on too much stress and adrenaline. He should've realized just how tired and vulnerable she was when he'd reached out for her at the lakeside and felt her tumble into his arms.

The memory of his lips brushing against hers sent sudden heat to the back of his neck. He'd been every bit as lost in the moment as she was and if Fitz hadn't started fussing, how long would he have held her there? Daisy was both physically and emotionally exhausted to the point of tears. She was running for her life.

What was his excuse? He didn't have one. He had to keep his emotions out of it, and taking her home to his parents was a good first step. Getting his parents' advice and getting Trent and Chloe to join them there were tied for second. Not that he knew yet what he was going to say to any of them.

His footsteps traced up the familiar path toward the farmhouse. Words played through his mind.

Hi, Mom and Dad. This is Daisy. She's on the run with a small baby, from both corrupt cops and gangsters after having witnessed a murder and finding some counterfeit money. There's a warrant out for her arrest, and Trent and Chloe are in a hurry to bring her in for questioning, so I was thinking she could hide out here until they got here. Obviously taking her to my place was out of the question, because I haven't cleaned in days and the corrupt cops stole my wallet. By the way, I kissed her. Yup, your bachelor son finally kissed his first girl, and I'm pretty sure it was the shortest kiss in history.

Damp filled the air as if the rain had gone back to hovering, just waiting to fall.

It was almost like a joke, the way Daisy had tumbled into his life, only not the funny kind. Because of his casual and laid-back manner, people assumed that he was a natural with women. But the truth of the matter was that romance had never been on his radar and he'd made it all the way to twenty-six without ever having kissed anyone. He'd even been proud of that fact.

But something about Daisy was different. There was an unusual physical beauty to her that twisted him up inside in a way no one ever had before, but it went way deeper than that. She was unmistakably tough. She had this odd combination of strength, courage and vulnerability all mixed together in a way that he couldn't help but admire and be attracted to. She was the first and only woman he'd liked this way, and she was probably going to get arrested by his brother.

The familiar shape of the house loomed ahead at the top of the path. The lights were out and his father's truck wasn't in the driveway.

Max climbed the front steps to the porch, settled Fitz safely under the wide front-window ledge, pulled his cover over him and tucked him in gently. Fitz gazed up at him, his eyes wide as if Max was the most remarkable thing he'd ever seen before. Max brushed his finger along Fitz's cheek. Yeah, he kind of felt the same way about him, too.

"Don't worry, little dude," he whispered. "We'll have you inside in a moment. You'll be able to stretch and play and get changed. We'll surprise my parents when they come home, and they'll absolutely love you. Now, just give me half a second, okay? I've got to find a way in."

He knocked twice on the front door and tried the doorknob. It was locked. He ran his fingers along the top of the lintel, feeling for a spare key.

Sneaking in and out the house had always been Nick's specialty. The littlest Henry brother had been a bit of a wild child, before something apparently happened at the end of high school that had scared him straight and made him turn his life around and enter the military. But back when they were teenagers, Nick had been an expert at crawling out of their window, down a rope he'd left tied to his bed frame. Max had tried it exactly once, slipped, broken his ankle and discovered that he found the inside of an ambulance way more interesting than whatever lame parties Nick had sneaked out to.

The footsteps behind him came so quickly he barely had time to spin around before he felt Daisy's body plow into him like a lithe quarterback. Her cry was fierce and wild, like the fighter he'd seen in her face that first moment their eyes had met. His body flew backward as his feet slipped on the wet wood. He tumbled onto the porch and Daisy fell on top of him.

Instinctively he caught her, one arm slipping around her waist and the other around her shoulders, pulling her into his chest and protecting her from the impact of the blow. He should've known she'd be scared and that she'd throw herself at anyone she thought could hurt Fitz. Even him.

"Where are we?" Daisy gasped. "Where have you taken me? Where's Fitz?"

She reared back, half sitting on his legs, with one hand pressed against his chest. Her other hand rose in the air, and he caught it before he could figure where it was about to land.

"This is my parents' house, and Fitz is fine!" His fingers tightened their grip on hers. "He's right over there on the porch behind us! I promise!"

Thunder crashed in the distance. He slid his legs out from under her, and she tumbled off him onto the porch. Her other hand rose, and he grabbed that one, too.

"What were you thinking?" she demanded.

"That my parents are really good people and we'd be safe here," he said. "My mom's a nurse, and my retired father runs free paintball events and shooting classes for youth groups. Fitz needs to be changed. You were fast asleep, and I figured I could go talk to my folks without you chasing me down and leaping on me like a warrior woman, ready to fight me to the death." He gasped and suddenly realized she was no longer fighting. She wasn't even trying to pull her hands out of his. "Apparently I was wrong. I should've woken you up. I'm sorry."

The front door flew open.

"Max?" His father's voice rose above him. "What are you doing?"

He looked up. Both of his parents were standing in the doorway. Mom's eyebrows rose. Dad shook his head. He couldn't begin to imagine how he looked, wet and tousled, sitting on his parents' front porch, holding both of Daisy's hands in his.

"Sorry I didn't call first. It's a long story, but both my phone and wallet were stolen." He dropped her hands just long enough to struggle to his feet, then he reached a hand down to help her up. She let him take it, and they stood there, like a couple of lost teenagers, holding hands on his parents' porch. "This is my friend Daisy. Daisy, these are my parents."

As if on cue, Fitz began to howl.

Max's mother unfroze first. She was a good foot shorter than her husband with a kind smile and shoulder-length hair that Daisy guessed had once been black and was now streaked with gray.

"It's very nice to meet you, Daisy," she said, reaching for her hand. "I'm Emily and this is

Maxwell's father, John. Welcome to our home. Please, do come inside and out of the cold. Max, will you fetch the baby? Sounds like he's in a hurry to get changed."

What had Max been thinking, bringing her here? She felt his fingers tighten in hers.

"It'll be okay," Max said, softly. "Like I told you, my parents are really good people."

She sighed. She didn't doubt they were good people. What she doubted was that Max had any idea what he was doing. He was a nice guy and a good man, but if what had happened back at the diner had shown her anything, it was that he was clearly in over his head. It was bad enough she'd put his life in danger. Her mess was now going to threaten the lives of his two apparently lovely and elderly parents, too. Thankfully, she'd got a long enough catnap to clear her head. It was about time one of them was thinking straight.

She pulled her hand away from his and shook his parents' hands in turn, making polite small talk as they welcomed her to their home and watching out of the corner of her eye as Max went and picked up Fitz. She couldn't help but wonder what Fitz thought of all this. For nine months, his view of the world had consisted entirely of his nursery and backyard.

Then again, her view of Canada had, too. They walked into the farmhouse.

"Where's the truck?" Max asked.

"We lent it to a neighbor," his dad said. "They're picking up a crib for their new grand-daughter today and needed something with cargo space."

Max wiped his shoes on the mat, ran both of his palms down the side of his jeans and searched his parents' faces with a look she couldn't read. "Has Trent called and filled you in on my little adventure?"

His parents looked at each other. It was a look that seemed to exchange endless librar-ies of shared knowledge in a glance.

"No, he hasn't," his father said. He closed the door and turned the lock, shutting out the cold and wet. "But I'm sure he'll be happy for you to call him. You can use my cell phone, if you'd like."

"I will," Max said, "once Daisy and Fitz are settled."

Her eyes drank in the large living room with overstuffed furniture and a wide, welcoming fireplace. Knickknacks and books spilled over the tables. Watercolors of flowers, farmlands, boys and a girl hung on the walls. Through a doorway, she caught a glimpse of a kitchen with a well-worn wooden table and dirty dishes for two piled by the sink.

Small talk floated around her, comforting and welcoming. Max's mother mentioned putting on a pot of stew for lunch, Max's father said something about baking a loaf of bread and then they debated for a minute where the children's old crib might be.

She couldn't stay here. She didn't belong here. These people with their perfect, happy little lives deserved better than the chaos helping her could bring.

Max undid the buckle that held Fitz in his car seat. Instinctively, her arms reached out, and she felt Max slide Fitz's small body into them. Her arms tightened around him.

"Don't worry," Max said, softly. "He's safe here. You both are."

He didn't get it, even after Officers Kelly and Bradley had shown up at the diner and threatened his life. She wouldn't be safe here. She wasn't safe anywhere. All she'd do was bring pain and danger into more good people's lives. Her chin rose. She turned back to his parents.

"Thank you for your kindness and hospitality," she said, "but Fitz and I can't stay here. I'll change him and feed him, and then we'll be on our way, once someone is kind enough to let me know how I can get my hands on a vehicle."

She watched as Max and his parents seemed to pass one shared look among the three of them, as if it was a hot potato they were each too polite to presume the other wanted to handle.

"Why don't you change your baby while I put the food on?" Emily said. "Then after everyone's had a bite to eat and the opportunity to warm up, we can sit down and help you figure out your next step."

Daisy almost smiled. Like mother like son, apparently.

"Thank you," Daisy said. "But you don't understand. I'm in trouble with police. Fitz isn't my child. I'm his nanny. I had to take him and run for my life from some very bad people, before they killed me and took him. His father begged me to take him and keep him safe, but for some reason the news is saying I kidnapped Fitz, and now I'm wanted for kidnapping."

She took a very deep breath. None of them interrupted.

"Believe me, I don't want to tell you any of this," she added. "I really don't. Especially since you're probably going to call the police.

But I don't want to lie to people as kind and good as you two seem to be. It's bad enough your son was accidentally caught up in all that and was kind enough to help me—even though he was robbed, attacked and had his life threatened trying to protect me. So please, after I leave, talk your son into forgetting about me. I don't want anybody else to get hurt."

Fitz coughed. She brushed her hand over his forehead. His fever was back.

"We know who you are, Daisy." Max's father spoke first. There was no smile on John's chiseled face. But there was warmth in his eyes. "We know who that baby you're holding is and something about the trouble you're in. We saw the news a few hours ago and joined hands to pray for you both, too. Not that we had any idea you had anything to do with our son, but we have a habit of praying for people on the news who need it, and it was clear that you and that precious baby were in some kind of trouble."

He glanced over to the door, and for the first time, Daisy saw the rifle resting above the lintel. John ran his hand over his jaw. "Of course, we never guessed this was how our prayers were going to be answered. But if our son showed up at our doorway with you, seeking sanctuary, then you're safe here with us, just as long as you give us your word that you're going to pray for guidance and talk honestly to our son and figure out how to do the right thing."

Unexpected tears rose to her eyes. Her mouth opened, but no words came out. She turned to Max, his eyes met hers and for one long wordless moment, they held each other's gaze with the same intensity their arms had wrapped around each other back at the lakeside. Fitz coughed again and then scrunched up his face and howled.

"Come on." Emily's hand brushed her arm. "I know you have a lot of important decisions to make. But any decision can wait until you've got cleaned up and had lunch. Let's you and I head upstairs with Fitz. He sounds like he needs to be changed and I'm guessing you could use a hot shower and a change of clothes, too. I'm sure I can find something close to your size."

Daisy broke Max's gaze and turned to his mother.

"Thank you," she said, but the words came out as barely more than a whisper. She blinked back her tears, and when they were too stubborn to move, she wiped them away with one hand. Then she let Emily lead her out of the living room, through the kitchen and toward the stairs heading up to the second floor.

"So, Dad, you think I should call Jacob and Nick and let them know that Trent and I have started a new family tradition?" Max asked when Daisy and Emily were halfway up the stairs. "Every Henry brother is required to bring home at least one damsel in distress."

She winced, guessing he hadn't meant for her to hear that. Emily winced, too.

"Forgive Max," his mother said. They continued up the stairs. "He likes to hide his feelings behind attempted humor sometimes. It's a bad habit and maybe it's partially my fault. I relied on him a lot when he was little. We all did. When things got too serious, Max was always the one who knew how to lighten the mood. I think sometimes he needs to be reminded that it's okay to be serious."

Daisy wasn't sure what that meant. The two women kept walking up the stairs, and the men's voices faded behind them. When they reached the second floor, four bedrooms spread out in different directions and another staircase led up to the third floor. Emily led her into a tiny bedroom with pale purple walls and a beautiful mural with a silhouette of a willowy girl with a shield and sword on the wall. One word was painted underneath: *Faith*.

"It's exquisite." Daisy's jaw dropped. "Who's Faith?"

"Max's sister," Emily said. The sister that Max had never once told her about, never once mentioned. Emily pulled an old blanket from a cupboard, folded it twice and laid it on the bed. "You can change Fitz here. I'll go draw a bath. I'm worried about his fever and his cough. A bath should help."

"Thank you," Daisy said again. "I don't want to cause you any trouble, and if there's anything I can do…"

Her words trailed off. The words felt so inadequate but she didn't know what else to say.

"Max puts on a brave face," Emily said. She glanced at the mural. "But he's got a pretty soft heart and for whatever reason, he's let you get your hands on it. Promise me you're never going to hurt him."

TEN

Max stood in the living room for a long moment, watching the empty space where Daisy and Fitz had been. Then he collapsed on the couch. His body sank into the soft cushions and a wave of unexpected relief moved through him, as if all the tension he'd been holding in his limbs had finally decided to release. It felt good to be back in his childhood home. He looked up at his dad.

"I like her," he said. "I know I shouldn't, but I do."

His father's eyebrows rose. They were kind eyes, Max thought, stern in the center yet with a certain softness that came from a long life marked with love, loss and compromise. John snorted. "I can tell, son. Just surprised to hear you admitting it to yourself."

Heat rose to Max's face. His father thought he'd meant he liked Daisy romantically? His hand ran over the back of his neck, and he felt the heat of it under his palm. Why on earth had he blurted that out? He must have been more tired than he thought.

"That's not what I meant," Max said. "I meant that I think she's a good person. She has a good heart and she loves that baby with everything she's got. She's just caught up in a bad situation and I want to help her."

His father crossed his arms and sat down in his armchair by the fireplace. "What do your brothers say?"

"I only talked to Trent and also Chloe," Max said. "He said to keep her safe until he can take her in for questioning and to stay off the grid. I need to call him and let him know where we are. We were supposed to meet them at a highway diner, but two other cops showed up and threatened me. Trent says that organized crime is involved. He's hoping he can convince Daisy to testify. The bigger problem is that Daisy doesn't know he's a cop, and she's going to hate me when she finds out. She doesn't trust cops, and honestly the more I know, the less I blame her for that. I'd hate cops, too, if I'd lived through everything she has. Trent specifically told me not to tip her off, and I get that he has his reasons, but to be honest even if

Trent hadn't said that, I might not have told her. I don't know. It's been a really crazy twenty-four hours."

Had it only been that long? Floorboards creaked above his head and then he heard the whoosh of water running through the pipes that meant someone was running a bath.

"Well, if you want my advice, you'd better come clean with her before your brother and Chloe show up." His dad stood. "The faster you tell her the truth, the faster she can forgive you, and that's important if you want to have any kind of future with her."

Future? Max laughed, because the thought was preposterous. He figured any single guy with half a brain would want a future with Daisy, just like most hockey fans dreamed of scoring the final goal to win the Stanley Cup. That didn't mean either fantasy would ever be within his reach.

"I don't know what you think is going on," Max said, "but Daisy and I have known each other for a day and we spent most of that on the run. Once Trent gets here, Daisy's either going to get arrested or lose her temper or both. Either way, I'm never going to see her or Fitz again, and there's absolutely nothing I can do about it."

No matter how painfully the urge to do something—anything—to save both of them beat in his chest.

His father paused with his hand on the doorway.

"Do you remember the story of how I met your mother?" he asked.

Max shook his head and wrinkled his brow. He was too exhausted to even guess where his father was going with this. "Only vaguely. It was a party or a church thing, right?"

"It was a bonfire barbecue for a friend's birthday," his dad said. "I saw her standing by the fire. We got to talking and there was just something about her. We talked the whole night, I walked her home, then when I got to the front door, I blurted out something foolish about how I thought I was going to marry her one day and asked if I could kiss her goodnight. She said no."

Max chuckled. So did his dad.

"She told me I wasn't allowed to talk about marriage again until we'd been dating for a year," he said, "and that we had to date for a whole three months before I could even try to kiss her again. Your mom was tough on me. But she was right of course. I was right, too, though. We got engaged exactly one year and one day later."

The sound of water shut off above them. A wry half grin crossed his father's face like he was looking at something that had taken place both a very long time ago and also yesterday. Max waited.

"I don't know what I'm saying, exactly," John said. "We were two college students at a party and it probably feels like none of that relates to what you're going through. Your mother is always better to talk to about relationship stuff. Or your big brother Jacob is pretty good, too, if you want a man's opinion. But if life has taught me one thing, it's this— there are things you just know. And when you know, you know. Now, I'm going to see if your mother wants me to do something with the soup. Call Trent."

"I will. Thanks, Dad."

His dad nodded and headed for the second floor. Max grabbed the phone.

There are things you just know. And when you know, you know.

What did he know, honestly? That Daisy loved Fitz. That she was brave and that she was innocent. And that yeah, if he'd met her at a bonfire instead of on the run from criminals, he definitely would've asked if he could walk her home. Maybe even tried to kiss her.

He dialed Trent's number.

"Hey, it's Trent." His brother answered on the first ring. Max was secretly waiting for the day his brother answered the phone so quickly he accidentally fumbled it and sent it flying.

"It's Max. We're at Mom and Dad's." Not that his brother wouldn't be able to read that from the call display. "Sorry I couldn't tell you more earlier, but as you know that line was not secure and could be compromised."

"Chlo'! It's Max!" Trent called, and Max heard Chloe breathe a sigh of relief. "You know she refused to go home until she knew you were safe? So we've just been hanging out and drinking too much coffee after, of course, taking the police officer we found at a crash site near Bleak Point into custody."

"Kelly, right?" Max asked.

"Officer Angelica Kelly," Trent confirmed. "RCMP."

"Did you take her to a station or the hospital?" Max asked.

"Hospital, for now," Trent said. "Under police supervision. EMT had concern over potential head trauma, but it's just a precaution."

Max suspected that was pretty much all he'd

ever hear about his potential kidnapper and patient. "What about her partner?"

"No sign of him yet. More important, do you still have custody of the baby and do you still have eyes on Daisy?"

"Yes and yes. They're both upstairs with Mom and Dad."

"So you really are at the house." Trent blew out a hard breath. "You brought a woman with a warrant out for her arrest to Mom and Dad's house?"

"Like you're one to talk! Need I remind you just how many violent criminals you brought here for Christmas?"

"Not on purpose!" It sounded like Trent's jaw was clenched. "It's not like I invited them all to come for Christmas dinner."

"Well, after my brother told me to lie low, I took my friend Daisy to the safest place I know, because she's in trouble and needed somewhere to go," Max said.

There was an awkward pause on the other end of the line, as if his brother was debating what argument he wanted to have. Max plowed on.

"As you've probably gathered, the diner was compromised. Two cops showed up. One of which you now have in custody. They said someone called an anonymous tip line saying I had sugar maple money."

Trent let out a low whistle. "You're serious? They called it sugar maple money?"

"Yup," Max said. Wow, seemed his brother was as into the stuff as the criminals were.

"But of course you didn't," Trent said.

"Oh, no, I had two hundred dollars of sugar maple money in my pocket," Max said, probably getting a bit too much enjoyment out of the volume of Trent's gasp. "Turned out Daisy found thousands of dollars of it in Gerry's car, then scattered it all around the cabin in order to slow Smith and Jones down."

Now he couldn't tell if Trent was laughing or coughing.

"This is not a joke," Trent said. "I know you like to be funny, but it's imperative that you're totally serious with me."

"I'm being dead serious," Max said. He stuck the phone in the crook of his shoulder and crossed his arms. "So you'd better tell me what's really going on and fast. Because Daisy matters to me and I'm tired of not being fully honest with her. Not telling her that you were a cop stopped making sense a couple of hours ago. So I'm going to tell her that my brother and soon-to-be sister-in-law are cops and on their way here. And you're going to tell me how I'm going to convince her to stick around and not run."

There was a long pause.

"As lead detective on this particular investigation, I'm authorizing you to be briefed on some of the details," Trent said. His voice snapped seamlessly from older brother to detective mode. "Sugar maple money is a very well done forgery that the RCMP has been tracking for about six months, although we believe it was first manufactured a little over a year ago. The new polymer currency that the Royal Canadian Mint rolled out back in the early 2010s was supposed to be impossible to forge. Someone somewhere created new software and technology to do just that."

"Wow," Max said. So Bradley might've been right that having sugar maple money in his possession was bordering on a felony.

"Yup." Trent sighed. "Off the record, the kicker is we didn't catch it until some botany student at the University of Ottawa emailed the mint and innocently asked when they'd replaced the little Norway maple leaves on the bills with sugar maple leaves. Then suddenly, overnight, everyone in the vice squad became an expert in exactly how many little pointy bits a maple leaf should have. Now the mint will tell you that the correct leaf isn't technically a Norway maple leaf either, but hey, I'm not a botanist. All you've really got to know is the counterfeit money has a maple leaf with fewer points."

"Sounds fun," Max said.

"Oh, it was," Trent said. "It wasn't my case, because I was getting ready to go undercover on a drug case, but I was in the loop. They thought they had a suspect months ago, but it fell through. They recovered a lot of electronic devices and memory cards, but they were all locked, and then some of them disappeared from the evidence locker. There was reason to believe someone working the case had been bribed or blackmailed to make it disappear, but it hadn't been proved. If we can convince Daisy to testify against her employer, that could be the break we need to crack this."

"But what if her boss isn't the forger?" Max asked. "Or if she doesn't know anything?"

"Then things get a lot more complicated." Trent let out a long breath and suddenly sounded less like a cop and more like an older brother. "We've been able to access the original 911 call that reported Daisy had kidnapped Fitz and proved the person used a doctored voice and a false identity, which is a very good sign. But we can't cancel the warrant until we talk to Gerry Pearce, and so far nobody's been able to locate him. Hopefully we'll be able to clear this up soon."

Max sank down at a kitchen chair. His head fell into his hands and his eyes locked on the old, familiar wood grain of the family dining table.

Lord, help me, please. Give me the strength to do the right thing.

"Tell me that you're not going to accuse Daisy of kidnapping Fitz."

"Max..."

"Promise me you're not going to arrest her."

"You know I can't promise that."

"Look, Trent, I know this is probably just another case to you! But not for me. I gave Daisy my word that I would protect her and Fitz. If my brother and his fiancée walk through this door, accuse her of kidnapping Fitz, rip that precious little baby from her arms and arrest her, she will never forgive me!"

He heard the stairs creak. He turned. Daisy was standing on the stairs behind her. Her face was white. Her hands were clenched in fists at her side.

"You're right," she said. Her voice shook. "I won't."

Her breath tightened in her chest. She walked down the stairs slowly, watching as the color drained from Max's face.

"I've got to go," he said into the phone, "I'll see you and Chloe when you get here." He set the phone down on the table and stood. "Where's Fitz?"

"With your parents," she said. "His teething fever is back and his chest doesn't sound good, so your mother is giving him a bath to help cool his fever and clear his congestion. Your dad said you needed to talk to me."

"I do." His arms parted, creating a safe place for her to step into. But she didn't step into his proffered hug. "And I'm very sorry, because I don't know how much of that conversation you overheard and I can't imagine how it must look. But I can explain."

"I don't want an explanation!" she said. "I don't want to stand here and listen while you spin some big convincing story to help explain away the fact that you just did the one thing I asked you not to do!"

Her chest tightened. She was struggling to breathe again. Just like she used to when her stepfather stood there and told lies about her to the police. Just like she had when she watched Anna die.

Was this why he'd brought her to his farmhouse? To trap her? To set her up? She'd been foolish. Her mother had trusted her stepfather. Jane and Anna had trusted Gerry. Her own ridiculous heart had trusted Max, and he'd betrayed her.

She pushed past him and ran through the living room, barely seeing the shapes of the furniture and things around her. Then she yanked the door back and stepped out onto the porch.

"Daisy! Wait!" Max called behind her. "Where are you going?"

Nowhere. She was going nowhere. Her hands grabbed the porch railing. Rain whipped her face. There was nowhere left to run. *Lord, I don't know what to pray right now. I feel so far beyond hope.* A sob slipped through her lips. Then she felt tears pushing hot and relentless through the corners of her eyes and rolling down her face, mingling with the rain, and this time, she let them fall.

Then she heard the creak of the wooden planks as Max walked out onto the porch. He stopped and she could hear him breathing, just a step or two behind her, and despite the pain and anger that filled her chest, something inside her wished she could just turn around and fall into his arms.

"My brother Trent is an undercover detective with RCMP Vice," Max said. His voice was soft and gentle, and it was like something inside it was begging her to listen. "His fiancée is a detective with the OPP's special victims unit. My eldest brother, Jacob, is also a cop, and my youngest brother, Nick, is in the military. I called Trent and Chloe for advice when you were at the motel paying for a cabin, because I was confused and didn't know what to do. I told him I was calling him as a brother, not a cop. He's the one who pulled in favors to get the diner open. He and Chloe were going to meet us there before Officers Bradley and Kelly showed up. I wanted to help you, Daisy. I didn't want to just leave you there."

"Well, you should have!" Fear, anger and regret crashed like competing waves inside her heart. "I asked you not to get involved. I told you to go. Instead you called your brother and his fiancée, so they could come arrest me!"

"So they could help you!" he said. "You told me that you would talk to the police if you knew with absolute certainty that they were good guys. You will never meet a cop more honorable than those in my family! If I hadn't called Trent, he wouldn't have known that Gerry had asked you to take Fitz and that whoever had reported Fitz kidnapped had done it apparently to flush you out. If I hadn't pleaded your case to them, told them how incredible you are and how convinced I am of your innocence, your case wouldn't be in the hands of a superb high-ranking detective who's willing to hear your side of the story!"

She turned toward him. He was standing just inches from her now and a sadness pooled in his eyes that was even deeper than the one that was crushing her own chest. For a moment, she almost felt her will falter, but she couldn't let herself fall into his arms again. Whether she'd meant to or not, she'd offered up her heart to him and he'd crushed it.

"I'm sorry," he said. "Believe me, I am. I wish I could go back, find the exact, right, perfect moment, and tell you who my brother was sooner. But I did what I thought was right. I did everything I could to protect you."

"I never asked you to protect me!"

"Fine." He stepped back and raised both

hands, palm up. "Do you want to keep running, Daisy? Really? Then go. I won't stop you."

"I don't understand."

"I think you do." He reached into his pocket and pulled out his keys. "You are not my prisoner, Daisy. I'm not your stepfather or Gerry Pearce. I'm not going to tell you that your only two options are to either stay here with me or walk off into the woods. If you want to leave, take my vehicle and go. Leave it somewhere safe and public, where it will be found and returned to me. Disappear, if that's what you really want. But I have one condition. Fitz stays here with me, until either Gerry or social services come to claim him. I will take care of him. I will do everything in my power to keep him safe. I won't let anybody hurt him and I'm pretty sure you know that's true. But I will not let you take him."

The keys lay there, dangling in the space between them.

"Do you think I should run?" she asked.

"Do you?" he asked.

No, she didn't think she should run, but she didn't think she should stay either. Thinking didn't factor into it at all. She couldn't remember the last time she'd done anything but act on the instincts that had kept her alive so far. "I don't know what to think."

His voice dropped. "Then what do you feel?"

Safe. The single word seemed to ricochet in her chest. She'd been furious with him. She'd yelled at him and battled against him with all her might. But instead of snapping at her or losing his temper like her hair-trigger stepfather or Gerry, he'd stood there and taken it. He'd let her yell at him. He'd let her be angry. He'd apologized for hurting her, even while she knew he was probably dying to defend himself.

And now, something about seeing him standing there, taking her fury and offering her his protection in exchange made her feel safe in a way she never had before.

"I don't want to run anymore." She grabbed his hand in both of hers and closed his fingers around the keys. He wrapped his other hand overtop of hers and she looked down at their hands linked together, with the keys dangling in between. "I want this nightmare to be over."

"Then trust me," he said.

Tears flooded her eyes. She dropped his hands and wiped them away. She couldn't believe he'd seen her cry. Nobody ever got to see her cry. "You must be so used to all this, rescuing people, watching them fall apart and getting involved in their crises. I overheard what you said to your dad about how rescuing women was now a Henry brothers tradition."

He put the keys back into his pocket and then ran his hand over his jaw.

"That was a joke," he said. "I didn't have a clue what to say to my father, so I said something silly. Believe it or not, it actually helps a lot at crime scenes to be able to calm people down, get their minds off what's going on and their fears of how bad things could be.

"But the last thing you want in a paramedic is someone who gets emotionally involved in anything. It's like this, you know how I told you about the shooting-and-paintball range my dad built? One year, he put these rolling logs in the pond. The trick was to run across them quickly without falling in. If you went fast enough, you were fine. But if you hesitated or went slowly, you'd fall. That's how I operate. Trent and Jacob get hunkered down into big, long cases. I deal with crisis after crisis quickly without stopping. I get people where they need to be and then I move on."

Except now. Except her. Something about this whole situation was different for him, and she didn't have the courage to ask him how or why. Because then she'd have to admit that it was different for her, too. She'd have to face the fact that the woman who never trusted anyone was standing there, a breath away from falling into the arms of the man who never let himself get emotionally invested and neither of them knew quite why.

"But why do you do that?" she said. "I know why I run. You know why I run. I was honest with you about my ugly and horrible past. But you haven't let me in."

"How can you say that? I told you all about my brothers. You're standing on the porch of my parent's house."

"But you never once told me about your sister."

"Because she's dead!" Max's voice rose until it cracked with emotion. "Because somebody killed my big sister, when I was three, and I don't like talking about it. Because whenever I do, it's like it hits me with this big wave of emotion that blocks out my ability to think about anything else."

Daisy's heart stopped. Max's eyes flickered over her shoulder and he shook his head. She turned. A white police vehicle was coming up the drive.

"I'm sorry," he said. "This is coming out all wrong and you deserve better than this. I wish I could go back to the start, do this entire thing over again and get it right. I just… I should've… I wish we had more time!"

So did she. His agonized eyes met hers. His hand brushed along the side of her face, tracing the lines of her features with his fingers before curling them deep into her hair.

"I've made a lot of mistakes," Max said. "But I know this might be our last opportunity to talk before my brother walks in and takes you into custody, and I might never see you again. So let me tell you this, Daisy Hayward. I've never let myself get involved in anyone's mess before I met you. I've never hugged someone deeply and held them in my arms. I've never brought anyone to meet the folks. I've never wanted to protect anyone or be their hero."

He leaned forward until his forehead pressed against hers. His voice dropped to a whisper. "And maybe this doesn't change anything, but I've never even kissed anyone before you. I'm twenty-six, and you're my first kiss. That's how rare and special a thing you are to me."

The rain tapered off again. Tires crunched closer on the gravel. The car grew closer. Her hands slid up around his neck and she felt his thick, soft hair beneath her fingertips. He pulled her to him.

Their lips met.

He kissed her like they both knew it was time for goodbye and neither knew how to say it. She kissed him back like he was her anchor, her pillar and he was the only thing keeping her from falling. They held each other as the headlights grew brighter behind them and swamped the porch, flooding them in the light. But they didn't break their embrace, until they heard a car door open behind them and a voice bark. "Hands up and get down on your knees! Both of you! This time you're going to talk or you're going to die. It's up to you."

She turned, feeling Max's right hand grab hers and hold it tight.

It was Officer Bradley.

ELEVEN

Instinctively, Max stepped in front of Daisy. Bradley was advancing, a gun in his hand, one eye puffy and black, anger smeared across his bleeding lip. Max's inner paramedic wondered if there'd been another car accident or if the corrupt officer had been in fight.

His eyes rose to the dark skies above and a prayer for everybody's safety crossed his heart. How long now until Trent and Chloe would be there? Twenty minutes? Twenty-five? If he managed to stall Bradley until they got there, they could arrest him. But if he did that, he'd be putting Fitz, his parents and Daisy in danger.

Lord, help me focus. Help me triage. What's important now?

He turned to brush his lips along Daisy's cheek and whispered in her ear.

"You and Fitz will be safe with my folks.

Dad's an even better shot than I am. You get inside the house and stay there. I'm going to keep him busy until Trent gets here."

He raised both hands and turned toward the corrupt cop hoping Daisy would do as he'd asked. But he could tell by the slight shake of her head and set of her jaw that she wasn't about to run. No, she was going to stand fast on his parents' porch behind him.

"Bradley, hi!" Max called. He stepped forward. "How's Officer Kelly? I heard she was in the hospital."

Worry flickered across Bradley's face, so quickly that Max almost missed it. Yeah, even criminals had people they cared for, something he reminded himself every time he saved a drunk driver's life.

"She's fine but she was arrested. I'm guessing thanks to you," Bradley said. The gun shook slightly in his hand and he steadied it with the other one. "They took her to the hospital and then handcuffed her to the bed."

Yeah, that matched what Trent had said, and while Max had mostly asked the question as a stalling tactic, it was odd, the palpable sense of relief he felt knowing that a patient who could've killed him was okay. He hated losing anyone. Even the criminals.

But if he'd thought for a moment that saving Kelly's life was going to make Bradley see the error of his ways, then clearly he'd been wrong. If anything, the look in Bradley's face was even meaner and more vile than it had been when he'd first waved a gun in Max's face.

Bradley gestured toward Daisy with the barrel of his gun. "Tell me who your friend is."

"Someone who has nothing to do with whatever trouble you've come looking for," Max said. "I'm guessing you're not here to apologize and give me back my phone and wallet."

"Ran into someone who wanted them more than I do." Bradley's tone projected more bravado into the words than the bruises and cuts implied.

"Let me guess, two big bald men with scars?" Max asked. The sneer on Bradley's face implied yes. So, Jones and Smith had his wallet and identification now. That was very bad news.

"How about you tell me more about Blondie here." Bradley leered.

Max felt his jaw set. He walked down the steps. "Why don't you tell me what the end game is for you here? You're going to threaten the lives of strangers until you get your hands on enough sugar maple money to throw away everything your badge stands for?"

Bradley sneered, "So, look who suddenly knows all about sugar maple money."

"Yup," Max said. Keeping him talking meant keeping him from shooting. "Called my big brother Trent and he filled me in on how someone managed to figure out how to make counterfeit versions of the new polymer notes, but before the RCMP could track that person down, a couple of dishonest cops got greedy and tanked the investigation. I'm guessing that whatever payout or deal they struck with the counterfeiters wasn't enough, though, so they decided to try to get the technology for themselves."

It was a workable theory, Max thought, but not a perfect one. He could see all the symptoms—Anna's death, Gerry telling Daisy to run, the money, the house blowing up, Smith and Jones, the corrupt cops, the real Jane who'd died and fake Jane's obsession with getting baby Fitz—but couldn't figure out how they all fit in one simple, elegant diagnosis.

"How about you shut your smart mouth," Bradley said, "and get in the car?"

"Okay," Max said. "I'll get in the car and go with you, and we'll have a big long talk about anything you want. On one condition. You take me. My friend stays here. This is about you, me and the sugar maple money. She has no part in this. Now, just let me say goodbye."

Would Bradley believe him and let Daisy go? Bradley didn't give any indication that he knew who she was. Max could only hope that either Bradley believed Daisy had nothing to do with the sugar maple money or that he thought taking a willing hostage was better than trying to take two unwilling ones.

Either way, Max didn't wait for Bradley to agree to his terms. He turned back to where, Daisy was still standing on the top of the steps of his parents' front porch, despite his entreaty for her to hide inside. Her skin was drenched in the thin beams of sunshine now filtering through the clouds and he knew without a doubt that she was the most beautiful thing he'd ever seen. She shook her head. Her dark eyes pleaded with him not to go.

Baby, you think I'd leave if I had any other choice? But I have to. I have to hope he'll agree to this. It's the only way.

"Daisy, it's going to be okay. Just talk to my brother when you see him," he said. "I trust you."

He trusted she'd stay there and wait for Trent

and Chloe. He trusted she'd tell them who'd taken him and give them a description of the man and his license plate. He had faith that he'd still be alive when they found him, and he'd be able to tell them how to patch him back up again from whatever this criminal decided to do.

He trusted Daisy would save his life.

He took a deep breath, prayed for courage and turned back to face the man who he knew without a doubt planned to kill him once he'd got everything he wanted out of him. Despite the fear, he felt a wry smile curl on his mouth. He was very good at talking for a long time when he needed to.

Bradley scowled, looking for a long moment from Max to Daisy. Then he waved his gun to her. "Girlie, come here. Nice and slow. No funny business, or I'll kill your boy here. I'm taking you instead."

"No!" Max raised his hands higher, palm up. "That's not how this works. I agree to go with you and cooperate. She stays here."

"You really believed me when I acted like I didn't know who she was?" Bradley asked with an ugly smile, and Max knew he'd been played. "You think I'm that dumb or that I haven't seen her face all over the news? She's got a warrant out for her arrest, which means it's my duty to arrest her. I know she used to work for Gerry and Anna Pearce, and that means she's tangled up in this somehow. Don't know how yet. Haven't figured that out. But I know she's valuable."

No, God, please help me find a way to stop this. I can't let him hurt Daisy.

But he could already hear the sound of Daisy's footsteps running down the steps behind him and then the crunch of her feet on the gravel. "Daisy, stop. Please. You don't have to do this."

"Yes, I do." She walked past him, with her head held high, toward the barrel of the gun. Her hands stretched out in front of her, the delicate skin of her wrists turned up toward Bradley, as she offered them up to him. He shifted the weapon to one hand. With the other, he reached for her hands, enveloping both of her delicate wrists in one of his. Then he yanked her forward, as if inspecting the merchandise he was just about to steal.

"You don't need him if you have me," she said. "I'm the one who worked for the Pearces. I'm the one who found the sugar maple money in Gerry's car and slipped it into Max's coat. He had no idea it was there. He's just a really good, innocent guy who got all twisted up in this mess somehow because he was trying to help. So leave him here and take me."

Bradley pulled her in so tightly she could feel the stench of his breath on her face. A greedy smile crossed his bleeding mouth, and his nose looked like it was freshly broken. But none of that was as ugly as the chuckle that came from his lips.

She used to think all men were like him underneath all the civility: selfish, greedy, out for themselves. Even Gerry Pearce, whose paranoia and mood swings she brushed off because at his worst he was still better than men like her stepfather.

But she'd been wrong. Because now she knew that no matter how much money somebody waved in Max's face or what threat or coercion they tried, his heart would always shine through.

She just prayed he trusted she knew what she was doing now.

"If you don't believe me, just reach into my jacket pocket and you'll find the cell phone Gerry gave me," she said. "He's been texting me constantly for the past twenty-four hours."

Bradley paused. She could see his mind

working and she prayed that his greed was stronger than either his patience or his logic. His hands tightened their grip on her wrists. Then he holstered his gun and reached for his handcuffs. Daisy headbutted him in the face as hard as she could and yanked both her hands from his grasp. Bradley howled in pain and grabbed his nose.

"Come on!" Max leaped forward and grabbed her hand. "We've got to run."

He pulled her off the driveway and into the thick bushes at the side of the house.

She gasped. "But what if he breaks into the house and hurts Fitz?"

Bradley yelled so loudly his swear words ran together in one long string of vile gibberish. Then a bullet sounded behind them, flying through the bushes near them like punctuation.

"Oh, considering how hard you headbutted him, he'll definitely chase." Max's hand tightened in hers. "Come on!"

They ran through the trees, plowing though the forest down a narrow, well-worn path. Behind them, she could hear Bradley swearing and shooting and crashing toward them.

The woods parted, and they rushed through a gate and into a maze like nothing she'd ever seen before. Old cars, boats, small houses and mannequins lay spread around the field with wild and abstract shapes. Ropes and bridges stretched above them, crossing over a pond to their right. A wall of buildings appeared ahead, like a historical fort or a western ghost town. And all around her, every square inch was coated in thousands of splotches of paint, forming a dazzling kaleidoscope of color. Max steered her toward a tower at the end of the row.

"Watch your head," he said, and she felt him brush a protective hand along the back of her neck as they pushed through a tiny wooden doorway. He pulled her against a wall. The room was narrow and at least two stories high, like a miniature grain silo. A rope ladder lay to her right with a crawl-height door on the opposite wall.

He slid past her and looked through the open doorway. "I'm afraid we've lost him. Which isn't good. I don't want him heading back to the house and getting any bright ideas. If he doesn't show up soon, we'll double back."

She nodded. "Where are we?"

"I told you my family built a shooting range and paintball course," Max said. She nodded. He had. But she'd never seen one before and never imagined anything that big or elaborate.

"We're in the paintball part. One of the two fort outposts, actually, that the teams have to defend. This place is half obstacle course and half little town. My dad spent two decades building this place. He lets camps and church groups use it now, but we still let out steam here when we're all up here together. I think it was his way of helping the four of us deal with the death of my sister. It was how he empowered us by teaching us to shoot and hide and strategize and defend ourselves. I remember every broken limb my brothers ever had and every single paramedic visit from my childhood, and this is where almost all of them happened."

There was a crash and then the sound of a familiar, bellowing voice. Bradley was outside. Max let out a deep breath. "Okay, here's what I need you to do. You're going to climb up this ladder to the top and come out in a small room. There's a huge metal crank in there. You're going to turn it and a big flashing light is going to come on."

"But then he'll see me!"

"Yup," Max said, "and he'll probably shoot at you, too. Thankfully, the plastic barrier surrounding the top is bulletproof, at least when it comes to what he's packing. Hopefully, he'll stumble in here and climb up the ladder after you. Wait until I set off the other flashing light beacon and then slip through the door to your right and start running along the tops of the buildings until you reach the second tower. There are bridges, nets and ropes to help you along."

The angry voice faded. Bradley was heading their way.

She shook her head. "You want me to make him chase me through an obstacle course?"

"Yes," he said. His lips brushed hers and then he guided her other hand to the ladder and held it taut to help her climb it. "You climbed out a second-story window with a baby, remember? You're going to lure him into a trap and I'm going to make him fall. Run as fast as you can and don't look back."

Bullets rattled the air outside. Sounded like Bradley had given up on trying to find them and was now just shooting indiscriminately. Max darted back out the door. She started to climb, feeling the rough wood of the rungs under her feet.

She pushed through a gap in the ceiling and ended up in a tiny room surrounded by a shimmering, near-invisible wall. Tiny sparks and flashes of light punctuated the course below her as bullets clanged and ricocheted off obstacles. She scanned the room and found a small metal crank. She turned it.

The light was red, blinding and instant, flashing on and off from the ceiling above her and swamping her body in its light. Bradley turned toward her, aimed his weapon and fired. She dropped to her knees and heard the thud of the bullets bouncing off the plastic shield surrounding her. Bradley ran toward the tower.

There was a trapdoor to her right leading to a series of rope bridges, netting and wooden planks connecting building roofs. A second tower like the one she now stood in lay at the very end. She couldn't see Max anywhere.

She heard Bradley burst through the door beneath her, then the sound of him climbing up the rope ladder. Her limbs tensed to run. She couldn't just stay there. She couldn't just stand in a tiny transparent room and wait to be captured.

Then she saw light flashing red and white at the other end of the course. *Thank You, God!* She turned to run.

A large hand grabbed her ankle and yanked her back toward the trapdoor. She kicked out hard and caught Bradley in the jaw. He let go, and for a moment, she thought he'd fallen, but then he braced himself with one hand, slid his gun through the hole and fired. But it was too late.

She'd slipped through the trapdoor and out onto the canvas bridge, weaving her way through the netting, using both hands to climb. She reached the end and crossed a long, narrow plank, before shimmying along a bridge, suspended by chains. Then she leaped down and sprinted across two rooftops and dived into another rope-maze bridge.

The gunfire stopped, but she could hear him coming after her, panting, wheezing and spitting out threats as he made his way through the course behind her. Bullets fired in the air, but he couldn't get her in his sights, not with the way the course twisted and turned. Every step seemed designed to be hidden from the one before. She kept her eyes locked on the flashing light ahead and prayed with every step that Max knew what he was doing.

A net spiderweb ended sharply at a wall. She dropped down five feet onto another roof and ran across it. A long wooden swing bridge spread out beneath her feet, like a ladder of widely spaced planks spreading over the pond as it curved up toward the lighthouse tower.

She could see Max now, his tall strong form at the other end, one hand outstretched, beckoning her toward him as the other turned the crank to maintain the beacon light.

She ran toward him, leaping from plank to plank as she felt them shaking beneath her feet. Then the weight of Bradley's heavy form landed on the bridge behind her.

"Stop! Right there!" he shouted. "I've got a clear shot, and I will take it!"

Her steps froze, her hands grabbing the rope bridge as her eyes locked on Max's form, just a few steps ahead of her. All she needed to do was leap up six more planks and she'd reach him. But Bradley was right. There was nowhere to run, nowhere to hide and a twenty-foot drop to a murky pond on either side.

"Daisy." Warning rumbled through Max's voice. "Keep running. Don't look back and don't let go."

"You take one more step," Bradley shouted. "I'll shoot you in the back!"

A bullet whizzed past her head. She turned and her hands gripped the knotted rope beside her.

The bridge gave way beneath her feet.

TWELVE

She fell, her feet sliding off the wood slats as her hands desperately tightened their grip on the rope. Wet knots dug painfully into her palms. Bradley howled as he tumbled into the dark muck of the pond below. She hung there, suspended between the sky and the ground, her feet scrambling for footing and pain shooting through her hands.

Then she felt a strong hand brush her shoulder.

"Come on," Max said. "Grab my hand. I'll pull you up."

She reached for him, detangling the fingers of one hand from the rope and sliding them into the warmth and safety of his grasp. He held her firm. She slid the other hand free, too, and grabbed for him, and only then realized he was hanging upside down, with one hand clutching a plank above her and his strong legs braced against the beams.

He pulled her up, her fingers brushing the strength of his muscles under the skin. Then they sat on the floor of the second tower, side by side, panting and listening to the sound of the man shouting beneath them.

"That water hazard is a doozy," Max said. "He won't drown, but he won't be able to pull himself out either, until someone helps him out or tosses him the ladder. There should be enough water in there to have cushioned his fall, so hopefully he won't have broken a limb or strained anything. I really don't want to have to carry him back to the house."

Her hand brushed his jaw. "You'd carry him all the way back to the house after he shot at us?"

"Yup," Max said. "Like I said, I don't get to pick and choose who I help."

A light flashed in the trees, bright against the cloudy grey sky. Max let out a laugh, leaped to his feet and turned the crank. The light in the distance flickered on and off. Max jiggled the crank back and forth, mimicking the effect.

"That'll be Trent and Chloe," he said. "I don't know what they're going to think when they get here and find I kindly trapped a sec-ond dirty cop for them. But believe me, I'll be teasing Trent about the fact we practically caught two criminals for him for years to come."

She watched as two figures drew nearer. Then she saw them. Trent was tall, with slightly broader shoulders than Max and a determined set to his jaw. Chloe almost matched him in height, with long red hair tumbling down her back.

"Don't worry," he said. "Trent was work-ing hard to contact Gerry, and I'm pretty sure they're not going to arrest you. Not if I have anything to say about it."

Max slid down the rope ladder to the bot-tom of the tower and ran across the course to meet Trent and Chloe. Her phone buzzed in her pocket. She pulled it out and glanced at the screen.

Gerry had texted four times, with updated directions on where he was and where she was to bring Fitz. Seemed he wanted her to head south and take Fitz to Toronto. At least that was closer than Sault Sainte Marie.

She quickly wrote back, apologized for being out of touch and told him that she hoped to bring Fitz to the meeting place by nightfall. The message was sent.

She'd texted what she'd hoped would happen, but she had no idea what would happen next. Would Chloe or Trent come with her? Or would they be the one taking Fitz to see his father? Would they arrest Gerry? Would the next time he saw his son be through prison bars?

And if they took Fitz, would they let her say goodbye?

She climbed down the rope ladder, out the doorway and then hung back as Max led the two cops over to where Bradley was still thrashing in the water and swearing. She watched for a moment as they arrested and secured him. The precision and professionalism of how they read him his rights and cuffed him was so very different from the way Bradley had blustered and threatened.

She couldn't imagine the relief they must feel, knowing two traitors in their force had finally been found and caught. She hoped interrogating Bradley and Kelly would lead to the arrest of Smith and Jones and tracing the origin of the sugar maple money.

An odd weight sat in the bottom of her heart. So this was it, then? It was all over. The police had arrived, they would take over and make sure Fitz was taken care of and that Jones and Smith would be stopped. This weird and wild adventure that she and Max had been on, running for their lives and escaping criminals, as terrifying as it had been, had also been the most exhilarating and purpose-filled thing she'd done in her life.

When she'd grabbed Fitz from his crib and run from the Pearce mansion, she'd not only saved his life, she'd finally done something that mattered with hers. And when Max had reached for her hand in the woods and asked her to trust him with Fitz, even if just for a fleeting moment, she'd known what it was like to imagine not having to go through life alone.

Now it was all over. And it was time to say goodbye.

She leaned back against the wooden wall, closed her eyes and prayed for wisdom.

Lord, all this time my gut has told me that Gerry wasn't a forger. But what if I'm wrong? Help me trust Max. Help me trust that Trent and Chloe are honest and not easily fooled, and that they'll make sure justice is done.

"Daisy!" Max was calling her name. She opened her eyes. Max strode toward her, flanked by Trent and Chloe. "Quick! They've got to take Bradley into custody, but they wanted to meet you first. This is my big brother Trent, and his fiancée, Chloe. Guys, this is Daisy."

There was a smile on his face when he said her name, broad and wide, like he was proud to know her. She swallowed hard and shook both cops' hands in turn.

It was clear in a glance that Trent and Max were brothers. Both had the same dark hair and proud shoulders. Though where Trent had a serious determination in his blue eyes, Max had a playfulness that glinted in his green ones. Chloe's handshake was firm, but there was a soft edge to her voice that implied all Daisy needed to do was say the word and the handshake would turn into a hug.

"It's very nice to finally meet you, Daisy," Chloe said. "We've heard a lot about you, and we have some very good news. The kidnapping warrant has been canceled. You're no longer under investigation."

Relief flooded her limbs. She grabbed Max's hand and held it tightly. He squeezed hers back and thanked God. She opened her mouth, but her words barely came out as more than a squeak. "Thank you."

"No problem," Trent said.

"I'm willing to cooperate fully in your investigation and that includes testifying against

Gerald Pearce," she said. Her chin rose. "I'm still not convinced he's guilty. But I trust Max, and Max trusts you. So I'm choosing to believe that you will do your jobs like honorable cops and that if Gerry's innocent, he'll be cleared. I have the phone he gave me and all the texts he sent me. I don't know much. But I'm willing to do anything I can to help in this investigation. Especially if it will help Fitz."

Trent's eyebrows rose. He looked at Chloe and they exchanged a long glance she couldn't understand.

"Gerald Pearce is dead," Trent said, gently. "He died in the explosion at his home yesterday."

The words hit Max's ears like boxing gloves. Instinctively, he slid his arm around Daisy's waist and felt her lean into it, as if her legs had suddenly been knocked out from under her.

"What do you mean, he's dead?" Max demanded. "Are you sure?"

Trent nodded and Max could tell in a glance how serious he was. "Oh, very sure. They've identified his dental records. He was shot and then his body was burned in the fire."

"But he's been texting me constantly since I left," Daisy said. She reached into her pocket, pulled out her phone and showed it to them. "See? He gave me this phone when he told me to run and take Fitz. He's been texting me the whole time."

The words faded on Daisy's lips as the implication of what she was saying hit her own ears, that whoever had been texting her wasn't Gerald and that all this time he'd been dead. Her hands shook. Chloe gently pulled the phone from her grip.

"We'll have our guys analyze it and figure out exactly who's been texting you," Trent said. "But I can assure you that whoever it was, it wasn't Gerald Pearce. They recovered three bodies from the house fire—"

"The news only said there was one body," Max interjected.

"Only one body was recovered initially," Trent said. "An adult male was found within the front door. The bodies of an adult woman and an infant were found buried deeper within the rubble. All were badly burned so it's been taking a while to identify the bodies. Not sure what's been released to the press yet. It was assumed originally that Anna, Gerry and Fitz Pearce all died in the fire, until someone called 911 and said that you had kidnapped Fitz and set the house on fire."

"Was it Jane?" Max asked.

Trent ran his hand over his jaw. "That's the name she gave."

"You said there was a dead baby." Daisy's face paled as the words fell from her lips.

"It was a hoax." Chloe's hand landed on her shoulder. "The infant was dead months or even years before the fire. The forensics guys took a second look at it the moment we heard from Max that Fitz was with you. They discovered it was a cadaver, who was several months older than Fitz and had died of illness. Our guys are now searching cemeteries in the Montreal area to see where it might've been dug up."

"Unfortunately, this mysterious Jane woman must've figured out that the ruse had failed and already called in the kidnapping hoax," Trent took up the story. "Our best guess is that whoever killed the Pearce family wanted to kidnap Fitz, so they brought the corpse with them, so that it would be discovered in the fire and people would assume he was dead."

"Wow," Max said.

"Oh, they tried to be clever." Trent couldn't hide the disgust from his voice. "But no matter how smart they think they are, we'll still catch them."

Chloe's hand hadn't moved from Daisy's shoulder.

"I know it's pretty horrible," Chloe said, softly. "But you're safe, and you saved Fitz's life. Focus on that. And we'll talk a lot more later back at the house."

Trent nodded to his brother and then slipped back to where he'd left Bradley handcuffed and fuming. The sigh of palpable relief that he'd heard Trent breathe when his brother had seen exactly who had been floundering around in the bottom of the family's muddy pond and realized he finally had his man had been matched only by the look of sheer gratitude in his eyes. It was only in that moment that it had hit Max just how worried and stressed his brother had been by this case and what it had meant to him that Max had come through.

Chloe's eyes met Max's for a long moment. "You got this?"

"Yeah, we'll see you back at the farmhouse," he said. He tightened his arm around Daisy. But as Chloe walked away, Daisy suddenly slipped out from under his grasp.

"Wait!" she said, "If Gerald Pearce is dead, what happens to Fitz?"

Chloe stopped. "Gerald Pearce has a sister in Alberta. We called her and she's flying out today to come take custody of Fitz. I'm sorry. I can't imagine how hard this is for you, Daisy. But everything will work out okay, and we'll do everything we can to help you. There are some great resources available to help victims of crime, and that can include helping you get back to England."

Max and Daisy stood there for a long moment and watched as Chloe joined Trent, and then waited as the two of them and a swearing Bradley disappeared back through the trees. They followed slowly, bending the wet grass beneath their feet and walking in silence, so close to each other that their shoulders almost touched. But she didn't reach for his hand, and he didn't know how to reach for hers. His heart was heavy, as was every word he thought of speaking, as they lay there uselessly on his tongue.

Finally, he saw the roof of the old familiar farmhouse that, despite his small apartment, he'd always considered home. Funny how he hadn't even thought twice about bringing Daisy and Fitz here. That somehow, in his own weird way, although he hadn't been able to say so, he'd wanted to welcome them into the place where he'd grown up.

No, more than that, he'd wanted to welcome them into his life.

"You said you were disappointed you hadn't got to do any sightseeing," he said. "I know it's not the CN Tower, the Parliament buildings or the Rockies, but how many tours of Canada include a random guy's family farm and the opportunity to trap a criminal in his family paintball course?"

A sob slipped through Daisy's throat. She buried her face in her hands, but not before he saw the glimmer of tears in her eyes. His heart plummeted.

"Hey, I'm sorry!" he said. "I was trying to lighten the mood. I don't know what's wrong with me."

"Well, I don't know what's wrong with me!" she said without lifting her hands from her eyes. "You don't get it. I don't cry. I never cry. Not when my stepfather hit me. Not when he had me falsely arrested. Not when I was kicked out. Now, ever since meeting you, it's like my tear ducts have broken and suddenly all they want to do is leak."

"Let me see, please." His voice dropped as he took her hands and pulled them from her eyes. Then he reached up and carefully, gently wiped away the tears that shone on her skin.

She had no idea how beautiful she was, did she? Whether she was crying or laughing or yelling at him or raising her chin in stubborn defiance. Every bit of her was gorgeous and real. "You don't need to hide your feelings from me."

Her eyes met his. She shrugged and he recognized the motion as a subtle and defiant way to deflect his compliment. He almost chuckled. Did she have any idea how alike they were? Both so stubbornly determined to push people away. Both so determined to deflect people's attempts to show affection. They were like two hearts of stone that crashed and banged against each other, setting off sparks.

"Well, you're used to watching people fall apart," she said. "I'm not used to doing it."

His eyes flitted over to where Trent and Chloe now stood on their phones by their car. He was so tired of feeling like they were on borrowed time.

"Yeah, you're right," Max said, turning back to face her. "People cry in front of me all the time. They also yell, curse, lie and beg. They kick me, punch me and threaten my life when I'm only trying to help. People throw all their emotions at me and hit me with everything they've got. I'm like an emotional punching bag, it's part of a paramedic's job and I let it roll off me. I never let myself feel any of it and I don't let it impact me…usually."

There was something about that word—*usually*—that had been so reluctant to be spoken he'd had to practically force it past his tongue. He wondered what it would be like for him, for both of them, to turn all that determination not to get involved with anyone into a determination to cling tight to another person and love them with all of their might.

"My mother says I was her perpetually happy child who never cried," he said. "I'm sure that can't be true, but it definitely feels like it is. It was more than just not crying, though. I was always level. I never get wound up about anything. I don't tend to lose my temper or yell or get emotionally invested. That's how weird meeting you has been for me. Before you, whatever was happening around me, good or bad, I just laughed it off and let it roll off me." His voice caught in his throat, as if suddenly hearing his words for the first time had jolted something in his brain. "Because that's how I handle what happened to my sister."

He took a deep breath, but again the words he wanted to say seemed to be stuck somewhere inside him, unable to break free. There was this dam, deep inside, walling him off from all those feelings that crashed and surged inside him, and he didn't know how to break through it.

He let go of Daisy and ran both hands through his hair. "I don't know what I'm trying to say. I'm sorry. I feel like all my words are coming out wrong."

She reached up, grabbed both of his hands and squeezed them hard. "Don't stop. Keep talking. I don't care if you get your words wrong, I still want to hear them."

He closed his eyes for a moment. An odd lump formed in his throat.

"My sister, Faith, was murdered when she was twelve," he said. "She was killed by a stranger, walking home from school. He grabbed her and tried to abduct her, she fought him off and died in the struggle before he could even take her anywhere. They never, ever caught the guy. Which I think is why Trent and Jacob take it so personally when they can't solve a crime.

"I was only a toddler when it happened. I don't really remember her. But the sadness my family felt at losing her, that grief, covered my whole childhood. Sadness was like this weird, gray mist that always floated around my home, just above our heads, and would just suddenly descend on us sometimes, slowing everything down and making people disappear into it. I never knew when it would hit. I'd be playing with my mom, and she'd just start crying. Or we'd be having family dinner, conversation would just stop and everyone would go silent. Holidays were the hardest—birthdays, Christmas, Easter and Thanksgiving."

Daisy squeezed his hands even tighter. He opened his eyes again, looked into her face and saw the family porch light that meant home reflected in her eyes.

"My mom always had a hard time at holidays, too," she said. "Very different, but still. It was the only time she'd talk about my father. First, she'd start yelling and breaking things, until it all got too much and I'd run off to the park or into town and just go wander the shops. Running out was like my way of hitting Reset, because when I came home she'd be calm again and it was like nothing had even happened."

"My mom would just get really quiet," Max said. "Now, Trent was a hothead. He'd lose his temper and run off to the barn and start punching the wall. My dad would go after him and calm him down. Jacob was always the peace-maker. He was the responsible one, who'd start clearing the table, take over the dinner or do whatever needed to be done. Nick would act up and be naughty to get attention, so Jacob would basically have to grab him by the scruff of his neck and make him stay put before he could cause too much chaos."

He chuckled, then he eased his hands from her viselike grip and slid them onto her shoulders. "We probably all sound pretty dysfunctional when I say it like that, all with our different ways of dealing with a horrible thing. But now when I watch families fall apart in grief at crime and accident scenes, it helps to be able to relate to them."

Daisy's hands slid around him and he felt her fingers brush the back of his neck. Shivers ran down his spine. He pulled her tighter.

"Okay, and what were you doing while all this was happening in your family?" she asked.

"I was the one making everybody smile," he said. "I got good at figuring out when the family was going to descend into grief and I'd try to stop it from happening. Sometimes it worked. It was like I was a superhero and grief was my enemy. I could sense the sadness was starting to descend so I'd quickly figure out the right thing to say to make everyone laugh. I learned to skip across the top of my feelings and not let myself sink into them. But it wasn't because I didn't feel things. It was because my feelings always seemed too big, too strong and too scary. I was afraid if I let them in, they'd flood over me and I'd drown."

He closed his eyes and brought his head forward until his forehead touched hers. He felt the soft rise and fall of her breath against his face. And as much as he wanted to kiss her, he knew it was more important that she heard what he needed to say.

"Maybe I'm just as scared now of feeling things as I always was," he said. "Because when I look at you, and I think about you and Fitz leaving my life, it feels an awful lot like drowning. I don't know what I'll do when you say goodbye. Maybe I'll cry like Mom or punch something like Trent or build something like Dad and then shoot paint at it. But whatever it is, it's going to hurt a lot, that much I know."

The farmhouse door flew open. A wail filled the night, loud and long and so heartbreaking, Max felt like his heart would split at the sound. Then he heard a single word, gasped from Daisy's lips, and it felt like someone had cranked up the pain past his breaking point. "Fitz!"

They sprang apart and ran for the farmhouse. His mother ran down the stairs toward him. Her face was pale and a screaming Fitz clutched in her arms.

"His fever's spiked, suddenly," his mother said, easing Fitz into Max's outstretched hands. He brushed his fingers across the baby's scalding skin and knew in an instant what he needed to do before his mother said the words. "You have to get him to the hospital."

THIRTEEN

The siren blared on the top of Max's paramedic vehicle, its long looping wail mingling in Daisy's ears with the agonizing screams of the tiny babe beside her in the back seat as the rapid-response unit sped through the countryside.

"Hold on, Fitz," she said, brushing her fingers along his fevered cheek. "Max is going to get us to the hospital, then we're going to get you some medicine and it's all going to be okay."

Emergency lights flashed above them. Max's hands gripped the steering wheel so tightly his knuckles had gone white. Her eyes met his in the rearview mirror for a fleeting moment. Her heart caught to see how they glistened with worry.

"It'll be okay," Max said. His eyes snapped back to the road. "Fevers can spike suddenly in little kids. It's usually nothing more than an infection and can be treated easily with antibiotics."

She let her gaze run over the tiny screaming infant beside her and everything in her heart wanted to take the pain away.

Lord, please heal his tiny body.

"What if it's something serious?" Panicked tears choked in her throat. "What if the low-level fever we thought was just teething was something worse? What if something is very wrong?"

"I told you I'd do everything in my power to protect him, Daisy, and I meant it." Max's voice rose above the sound of the siren and Fitz's tears. "I know how special Fitz is. I care about him, too." He wiped a hand over his eyes. "I'm going to take care of him. I promise."

The minutes ticked by at agonizingly slow speed, each second seeming to stretch into minutes. Finally, she saw buildings appearing in the distance and the bright blue of a hospital *H* shining above them.

Max pulled the truck into the paramedic bay, grabbed his uniform jacket and forced his arms through the sleeves. She pulled Fitz from the car seat and they ran into the hospital. Her footsteps faltered as they ran through the sliding doors into the emergency room.

The chaos of caregivers and those needing care surrounded her on all sides in a sea of worry. She barely noticed when Max slipped away and had a quick word with the nurse behind the front desk. A moment later, he was back. He reached for Fitz.

"I can take him straight in," he said, "and we won't have to wait. Even though my wallet was stolen, I still have my badge, and they know me well here. I can take him right back, get him diagnosed and on the medicine he needs. But only if I take him in alone. I'm sorry, you're not a relative or legal guardian, and while your warrant may have been canceled, they still have your name on an alert list because of the coverage the kidnapping charge got. If Fitz's parents were still alive, they could grant you access, but under the circumstances, getting you authorized to come back with him will take both paperwork and time."

What was he saying? Fitz was screaming in her arms, clinging to her. Hot tears filled her eyes. And here was Max, standing there calmly telling her he was taking him.

"Don't make me give him up," she said. "Not

like this. Not while he's screaming. Not while he's in pain. Please. You don't understand."

But lips set in a firm line. A look filled his eyes that was so calm, it jolted something inside her.

"Yes, I do," Max said. "This is my job, Daisy. I can take Fitz straight to a doctor and get him the diagnosis and medication he needs. Delaying his admittance until you've been cleared to go with him isn't fair to him. Every second counts right now. Please, Daisy. You've trusted me before. Trust me again. I'll take care of Fitz like he is my own son. I promise."

He pried Fitz from her hands, pulled his screaming body up to his chest, and all she could do was stand there and let him take him.

"Chloe will be here soon," he said. "She's just helping Trent book Bradley, and then she'll be right over. Chloe hopefully will be able to help you get access, and I'll make sure someone is out for you as soon as I can. But not right this second and not until I take care of Fitz. Wait for me. Trust me."

She felt herself nod. Max turned and ran through a pair of double doors. Tears filled her eyes. She pushed through the emergency doors back outside to the sidewalk, staying close enough to the emergency room that she could see Max when he came back through but far enough away from those in need that she wasn't taking anybody's seat. A narrow rural highway ran past the hospital entrance, hemmed in by thick forest on the other side of the road. She sank down on a bench, pulled a thermos of soup and a hunk of fresh bread from the lunch bag Emily had given her and had a little of each without tasting either.

She'd never been in an emergency room before, not that she could remember anyway, and there was something overwhelming about the chaos, pain and need that had seemed to surround her on every side. The sick and the injured, the crying and the praying, those rushing at full speed and those shuffling slowly, these were the people that Max saw and cared for every day. This was his world and she couldn't imagine how he processed it all and kept his head about him, while he and those like him did the job of a hero, day after day after day.

She finished her lunch, wrapped her arms around herself and prayed. She prayed while ambulances and rapid-response units came and went, and people rushed through the doors. She dozed in and out, under the grey and cloudy sky, watching the trees sway in the wind, and sitting up like she had so many nights when she'd sat up, holding Fitz to her chest while he drifted to sleep. Until eventually, a nurse stepped outside the door and tapped her on the shoulder.

"You're Daisy Hayward, right?" he asked. She nodded. "I've been asked to let you know that the baby you came in with is responding well to antibiotics and sleeping soundly. Would you like to go see him?"

She leaped to her feet. "Absolutely! Yes."

She followed the nurse back through the emergency waiting room, down a long hallway, into an elevator and out onto a surprisingly bright and airy floor. He led her down the hall, past a string of hospital rooms, until they reached a room at the end of the hall. "Here you go. Your friend's in here."

She stepped into a large, private hospital room. It didn't make sense. How would Max arrange for a private hospital room? She didn't expect he'd have either that power or that amount of money. "Hello?"

"Come on in." The voice was crisp and female, with an oddly familiar tone. She took another step into the room and saw a woman with short black hair sitting with her back to her in a rocking chair between the window and the crib. She was Fitz's aunt, she had to be, and she'd come to take Fitz away.

Daisy took a deep breath and felt the door close behind her. She crossed the floor and saw Fitz, looking tiny and exhausted, lying in the crib with his face thankfully free from fever. She brushed her fingers against his cool, soft cheek.

"Thank you for letting me see him," she murmured. "I'm Daisy."

"I know." The dark-haired woman rose and turned.

Daisy's heart stopped.

It was Anna. Her lips tweaked with the familiar half sneer that implied the world was full of minor irritations and Daisy was the smallest of them all.

"But I thought you were dead!" Daisy's voice rose. "I saw you die."

Anna sniffed.

"Lower your volume. We're in a hospital, after all," she said. She pulled a tiny handgun from her pocket, intricate and lethal, and waved it in Daisy's direction as if she was swatting a fly off the back of her hand. "Uncross your arms and stand up straight when I'm talking to you. The whole point of choosing a nanny from England was that you were supposed to be a quiet little thing with good manners."

Daisy's fingers slid into Fitz's curled fist. He held her tightly.

"Yes, of course you saw me 'die,'" Anna said. "That was the point. You were supposed to see the house being trashed, witness my death and run out. Then after the explosion, you were supposed to tell the world that you saw me die and then go off back to your little life in England none the wiser. That was your role. Instead, you grabbed Fitz and ran off with him. I should've known. You've always had an unhealthy attachment to that little brat."

Daisy felt her chin rise. *Lord, maybe I should be afraid right now. But all I feel is fight and the determination to save Fitz. Help me get him out of here alive.*

"It was you," Daisy said. "You somehow talked Jones and Smith into murdering Gerry and setting the house on fire, because you wanted to steal the counterfeit technology he designed for yourself."

"Excuse me?" Anna's lip curled. "You think Gerald Pearce designed the counterfeit technology? You think he ran the operation or that Smith and Jones were ever loyal to him? I was one of Pearce Enterprises's head designers!

I replicated the bills and designed the technology, back when I was working under him. At first, having a relationship with him was enough to keep his suspicions at bay while maintaining unfettered access to his company and equipment. But he found the operation and got suspicious. He started taking pieces of my technology and files out of the office and hiding them on locked devices. I had to resort to low doses of poison to slow down his mind, but it only made him paranoid and erratic. One night, he called the police, and I was forced to bribe them to look the other way. He'd felt so guilty about our affair after Jane's death, he would've reassigned me to one of his other offices if I hadn't managed to convince him that the best thing to do for little Fitz was to marry me."

"So you could keep working on refining the counterfeit process right under his nose," Daisy said. "Did you kill Jane, too?"

"Don't be ridiculous," Anna said. "I don't like hospitals. That was Smith."

Daisy looked down at Fitz and her hand brushed over his tiny one as she promised herself silently that no matter what, she would protect him.

"How can you possibly think you're going

to get away with this?" Daisy asked. "I won't let you. I'll tell the police."

"Tell them what exactly?" Anna laughed. "That you saw the woman you work for, injured and bleeding on the floor, and instead of calling anybody for help, you kidnapped a baby and ran? Tell me, do you know how to prove I had anything to do with sugar maple money or Gerry's and Jane's deaths? Of course not. No one will believe you and you'll look like a lunatic. So no, you'll do no such thing. Instead, you'll be thankful that I've decided I'm keeping you on as Fitz's nanny. Whether I like you or not, I need to take him with me and you've clearly bonded with him. And I can't be expected to deal with a baby myself, especially a sick one who needs constant care and antibiotics. Searching for a new nanny right now would be a ridiculous risk for me to take, and I can't exactly delegate him to Jones and Smith to take care of. So you're going to go tie up an unfortunate loose end for me, then you're going to come back here, pick up Fitz and carry him wherever I tell you to go."

"Why?" Daisy asked. "What do you possibly want with Fitz? You don't like him. You don't care about him. Why can't you just let him go to be with a family who will love him the way he deserves?"

"Does it matter?" Anna asked. "I'm taking Fitz, whether you like it or not. The only question is whether he's traveling in your arms or in whatever baby container or carrier I can find to put him in. Now, I have one last task for you to perform before we leave. You didn't just make a mess of this whole thing, you got somebody else tangled up in it, too. Unfortunately, he's apparently now scouring the hospital looking for you, and when he finds someone moved the baby as well, he'll probably go frantic. Killing a man in a public place is not exactly the kind of attention I need, but having him running around making noise won't do either."

Anna glanced down at her phone. "Jones has a high-powered rifle trained on your friend Max right now. You're going to tell Max you're leaving. You're going to tell him whatever lie you need to tell him to convince him to drop this matter and forget he ever met you and Fitz. Then you can come back here, pick up the baby, and we'll go. I will be listening in, and you will make it convincing. Otherwise, I will give the order and Jones will kill him."

* * *

Max's gaze darted around the crowded hospital emergency room, scanning for the one unmistakable face in the crowd. People seemed to be everywhere, in a moving symphony of care, compassion and need. He didn't see her anywhere.

"Max!" Chloe ran through the hallway. Her voice was both gentle and sisterly, and as much as Max usually appreciated both qualities about her, right now it made him worried that he wasn't going to like whatever she was about to say next. "I've checked every ladies' room. Is it possible that Daisy's left?"

"No, it's not." Max frowned. He refused to believe it. Daisy was done with running and she'd agreed to cooperate with the police. She wouldn't just take off. And if she had, then what did that mean?

Trent's hand landed on his shoulder before Max even realized he'd returned from searching outside. Trent steered him toward the wall.

"Look, bro," Trent said, "I know you care about this woman, but I think you do need to face the possibility that she ran."

"She wouldn't just leave Fitz," Max said. "Not without a really good reason. Not without knowing he was okay. She loves that baby more than anything." Unless he'd driven her away. He ran both hands through his hair. "I think I might've been sharp with her. She was just panicking about Fitz and letting him go, so I made it very clear she was wasting time and needed to let me take him. What if I hurt her feelings?"

Trent's eyes grew wide, he took a step back, and then he and Chloe exchanged a long glance that didn't make Max feel any better.

"What?" Max said. "What's wrong?"

"Sorry." Trent ran his hand over his jaw. "We honestly had no idea the situation had got that serious."

"What situation?"

"Whatever this is going on with you two," Trent said. "Look at you! I just walked in here from booking a criminal who tried to murder you, there are more criminals out there who probably want you dead, and you're panicking that you hurt this woman's feelings! Which..." He blew out a long breath. "Which I can't even pretend I don't understand. It took me far too long to admit to myself that I was in love with Chloe, and you should've heard the way Chloe and I used to bicker and snap at each other."

"Although," Chloe said, "to be honest, it was usually because we were running for our lives and somebody was shooting at us. But it's true your brother gets on my nerves more than anybody else I know."

Trent slid his arm around Chloe's shoulder. "And she gets on mine, which is why she insisted we have a yearlong engagement and premarital counseling to give us the best possible head start. The bottom line is, I don't know if you hurt Daisy's feelings. It was a crisis situation, those tend to get everyone heated. If you did and she ran instead of even giving you an opportunity to work it out, then she's not the woman for you. Because I know you don't like drama and you like to pretend you're all chill. But if you want a future together, you're both going to make a ton of mistakes, and you have to get used to working them out and forgiving each other."

Funny how their dad had said pretty much the exact same thing.

Lord, I need wisdom and clarity. Help me see what matters most. Help me know what's important now.

A flash of gold caught his eye through the crowded room. Daisy was walking toward him slowly, her face every bit as calm as the moment they'd met, when Smith had her kneeling at gunpoint, and her dark eyes locked on his face like nothing else mattered. A breath left his chest so suddenly it was like the air had been knocked from his lungs. He strode through the crowd toward her. His arms opened wide, she tumbled into his chest and he held her there, feeling her heart beating against him and his hand running over the back of her head.

"I thought you'd left," he said.

She took a step back, her gaze running over the huge emergency room, as if she was scanning for one specific person or point in the crowd. When she spoke, it was almost as if she was talking to herself. "There are a lot of people in here. Kids, elderly people, injured people, doctors and nurses…" Her voice trailed off and it was only then he realized how very pale her face was. "Let's step somewhere a little less public. Like outside the front door."

"Okay," he said. "No problem."

He took her hand and led her out through the crowd toward the front door. His brother and Chloe hung back at first until, to his surprise, Daisy waved a slight hand in their direction, and they pushed off the wall and followed behind.

The double glass doors slid open with a familiar hiss. Daisy pulled him against the wall.

Both of her hands grabbed his. Her eyes darted over his shoulder. He turned and saw nothing but bushes.

"Don't say anything, please." Her eyes locked on his face. "I need to say something and I need you to listen, okay?"

He nodded. She said the words like he was a stranger. The beautiful spark that lit up the dustiest corners of his heart was gone from her eyes. He didn't know what had happened to the Daisy who'd been tenaciously pulling and tugging on his heartstrings ever since they'd met. He just knew he'd do whatever it took to get her back. "Talk to me. Please."

"I'm leaving." The two words slipped from her lips and hit him like a one-two punch. "Not because I want to, but because I have to. I can't tell you where I'm going and I don't want you to try to find me or contact me." Her lip quivered. "Please, Max. I want you to walk away and forget me."

"How can you say that?" He wrenched his hands from hers. "How can you possibly ask me to forget about you?"

She pressed her lips together as if trying to stop her chin from shaking.

"Because I need you to!" Her voice rose. "I don't belong in your life. I don't belong here.

I'm just some accident, some mistake, that fell into your path!"

"You're making it sound like you're something random I tripped over!"

"Well, maybe I was!" Sudden fire flashed in her eyes, flickering like flames at a pile of kindling. "Maybe that's what happened. You were going along in your life, happily and comfortably trying to get from Point A to Point B, and then suddenly I landed in your path and knocked you down. Now it's time for you to get up, dust yourself off and get on with your life."

"Maybe I don't want to get on with my life!" His hands rose like he was conducting a wave even as it crashed over him.

"You don't get that option!" Daisy said. "Because no matter what you say right now, I'm leaving and there's nothing you can do about it."

Doors hissed open and shut behind them. Sirens sounded as ambulances came and went. People rushed around on all sides. But there she stood, this one strong and fierce anchor in the middle of the storm. And suddenly he knew, without a doubt in his mind, that he was tired of trying to outrun the storm or skip over the top of it, like the messy things of life didn't matter. He wanted to be right in the middle of it. As long as it meant being there with her.

"What if I found a way to keep you in the country?" Max said. "I don't know how this works. But what if I helped you with a visa? I know you've just lost everything that anchored you here. But what if I was that anchor. What if I sponsored you? What if we made a go of it and tried to build a future together, like some of those lumberjacks and British governesses in those books my mother reads?"

"What if we make a go of it? What if we build a future?" Daisy's hands rose to her lips. Tears filled her eyes. "Why are you saying this?"

Because foolishly blurting out to a woman I just met that I'm suggesting a marriage of convenience in the hopes she'll one day fall in love with me is too ridiculous to say out loud. But what can I do, Daisy? I think I might be falling in love with you, but I've never said those three little words to anyone before and I'm not sure how.

He took her hands and slid them around his neck. But instead she pulled her hands from his and let them fall.

"Don't you dare joke about something like that," she said. "Not about this. Not about us.

If you don't get what you mean to me, then I'm glad I'm leaving. Because I'm not some damsel in distress. And if I ever do agree to build a future with someone, it will be because they can't imagine life without me and I'm not willing to live without them." She pushed him farther back and stepped out of his arms. "Goodbye, Max."

She turned and ran back into the emergency room. The doors hissed shut behind her.

He groaned. What had he done? Why couldn't he have just been honest with her? Why couldn't he have told her how he really felt? He closed his eyes.

Forgive me, Lord. Daisy deserves a man who's willing to fight for her. Help me be that man.

"Daisy! Wait!" He took two steps. She stopped, turned and looked back at him through the glass. His heartbeat pushed him forward but somehow his feet stayed still, as if afraid taking another step would spook her. "You matter to me," he called, "and if I need to spend months or years convincing you that I want you in my life, I will. All I know is that I don't want to lose you."

Daisy's eyes met his through the closed glass. Something glistened in their dark depths that made his heart pound with more hope, fire and happiness than he ever hoped to feel. It was that same gaze that had been in her eyes when she'd looked at Fitz. That expression that said she'd cared about the person she was looking at so much she was willing to fight for them and didn't want to lose them. "I don't want to lose you either."

"Then don't go. Stay. And we'll figure this out."

The smile fell from her lips. Then a red laser point of light flickered on the glass. "Max! Duck!"

He dropped to the ground as the emergency room doors shattered.

FOURTEEN

"Shooter!" Trent bellowed, running for the trees. "Everybody down! Chloe! Secure the hospital!"

Max rolled, sheltering his head as safety glass rained down around him. What was happening? Where was Daisy? He rolled up on one elbow and watched as his older brother raised his weapon and fired a precision shot across the highway and into the forest. A large man in camouflage fatigues tumbled from a tree. It was Jones.

Max's heart pounded with prayers of thanksgiving. If Jones hadn't aimed right at him, others around him could've been injured; if the safety glass hadn't slowed down the bullet, people inside the hospital could've been hurt; and if Trent hadn't been there, Jones wouldn't now be facedown on the ground.

Most important of all the ifs was if Daisy

hadn't warned him to duck at that exact second, the bullet that had flown over him would've pierced him through the core without a doubt. His hand slid over his heartbeat. How long had she known there was a weapon aimed at his heart? Was it why she had said goodbye?

He had to know. He had to find her. He climbed to his feet and searched the scene. Chaos swirled around him. Chloe was working to help secure the building. Trent was arresting Jones, who'd survived his fall, even as paramedics rushed toward the criminal to patch up what looked like a broken leg and a gunshot wound to his shoulder. Nurses and doctors were working to get people away from the glass and make sure everyone was all right. Max had only one job to do—only one thing that mattered.

He had to find Daisy.

He yelled to his brother. "Trent! I'm going to—"

"I know. Go, get her!"

A determined smiled crossed Max's face. He slipped through the shattered door, his eyes meeting Chloe's as she directed him past security. "Where did she go?"

"That way." She pointed to a stairwell. He

ran for it, hearing her voice echoing behind him. "I'll be right behind you as soon as I can!"

He was thankful for the offer of backup, but there was no time to wait. He pushed through the stairwell door and started running up the cement stairs, taking them two at a time. Daisy's screams echoed in the stairwell above him. By the sound of things, she wasn't giving up without a fight.

Bullets sounded down the stairwell toward him, clattering against the railing, chipping away the corners of the steps even as his feet skimmed past them. He pressed his body against the wall. Gunfire poured down the stairwell. He took a deep breath.

Now what? He couldn't run up into gunfire. But if he lost them now, he might never find them again. *Lord, what do I do?* Then he heard Daisy's voice, floating down to him above the chaos like a light shining in the darkness calling him home. "Tower beacon!"

Her voice stopped short in a yelp, but she'd given him all the information he needed. She was headed to the roof.

Bullets flew past his face, clattering down to the bottom of the stairwell. Below him he could hear the door on the ground floor open and shut, as if Chloe had been about to follow him but had been unable to make it through the door.

Max slid along the wall to an emergency door, burst through and came out on the maternity ward. He ran through the floor as quickly and safely as he could, praying with each step that he'd understood and that he'd been right. He threw himself through another door and pelted up the stairs, his strong legs forcing him upward. Then he pushed through onto the roof.

Gray clouds lay heavy above him. An air-ambulance helicopter, like the ones he'd ridden in hundreds of times before, hummed ahead of him, its propellers spinning in preparation for takeoff. He drew closer.

A solo figure with bulky shoulders and a bald head sat at the controls—Smith. The back door lay open. The cabin seats were empty, but the cabin itself was full of cardboard boxes, stacked around the usual long stretcher and paramedic equipment. Max risked running closer. The crack of a bullet made his footsteps freeze. He turned in time to see a dark-haired woman turn the barrel of her small handgun back to the blonde woman standing beside her and the small baby clutched in her arms.

It was Anna Pearce, alive, smirking and pointing a gun at two of the most amazing people he'd ever met. His eyes met Daisy's and she held his gaze, steady and brave, despite the fear he saw brimming in the depths of her eyes. Fitz howled, his face buried in Daisy's chest, and Max knew, without a flicker of doubt in his mind, that he would do anything in his power to save them.

"Anna!" he called, raising his hands and nodding slightly. "I see you're not as dead as the news is reporting. Or should I call you Jane?"

"Just a little immature joke on my part, I'm afraid, to use the name of Gerald's beloved late wife," she said and her smirk twisted more cruelly. "He genuinely did love her, I think. He was fascinated with me, but fascination only lasts so long."

She walked Daisy and Fitz toward the helicopter. "I should thank you for providing your wallet, phone and ID to Officer Bradley. It made getting Fitz out of the hospital and borrowing a helicopter much easier. But I see you didn't take my advice to leave Miss Hayward alone, just like she didn't obey my direction to convince you to leave."

"No, ma'am!" Max called, turning his eyes to the beautiful blonde holding the precious baby in her arms. "I'm afraid there's just something about Daisy and Fitz that makes them impossible to leave."

Anna stopped. Her gun flickered from the soft skin at the side of Daisy's temple, then down to Fitz's head, and Max watched as pain filled Daisy's gaze. "What if I gave you a choice? Whose life would you save? Daisy's? Or Fitz's?"

Agony filled his heart so quickly it yanked oxygen from his lungs. Was she honestly giving him a choice? To save one and let the other die? How many times had he been forced to make that choice? Who to help first? Who to save?

But even as the questions swamped his mind, his heart knew there was only one answer to the question.

"I would not choose," he said. "Because I don't want to live without Daisy, and Daisy doesn't want to without Fitz."

Something dark flickered in Anna's eyes, disappointed perhaps that he wouldn't play her game. She shoved Daisy toward the helicopter's open back door and gestured at her with the gun. He watched helplessly as Daisy struggled to climb into the back of the helicopter with Fitz in her arms, until Smith left the cockpit, grabbed her by the shoulder and yanked her inside. He pushed her back into a seat. She buckled the seat belt over her chest. The large bald thug went back to the cockpit.

Anna's laugh was swallowed up by the sound of the rotor. "I'll tell you a little secret, Max!" she shouted. "I need Fitz. My good-for-nothing dead husband's deceit made sure that I would need him, and I'm counting on the fact your little Daisy is going to protect Fitz with her life for me, no matter what I do."

He didn't know what that meant or what this cruel, mad woman would need with a tiny baby. Anna laughed and shouted something else, but her words were lost in the sound of the rotors speeding up. Daisy cupped her hands over Fitz's ears and cradled him tightly, sheltering him from the noise. Anna strapped herself into a seat across from Daisy.

Max ran toward them. But it was too late. The helicopter began to rise.

Four feet.

Daisy's eyes met his, wide and filled with fear.

Six feet.

Anna turned her back to them and shouted something at Smith.

Eight feet.

I love you, Daisy. I'm sorry I didn't know how to say it earlier.

Her chin rose, her lips moved and he read her silent words. *Max, I trust you.*

Ten feet.

His arms stretched out toward them. She brushed her lips across Fitz's brow. Her eyes met Max's. *Catch.*

Then she dropped Fitz out of the helicopter toward his waiting arms.

A sob left her lips as she felt the precious child she'd cared for ever since she'd come to Canada slip from her hands and fall into Max's outstretched arms. Fitz's wail wrenched a hole in her heart. But even as she watched Max reach for him, a deeper peace than she'd ever felt before filled her lungs. Max would keep him far safer than she could.

Fitz tumbled into Max's hands. His protective arms tightened around the frightened child, cradling him to his chest. Fitz shuddered a sigh and nestled into Max's chest. Daisy closed her eyes and felt the tears slip her lids as the helicopter rose.

Thank You, Lord. Thank You that Fitz is safe in Max's arms. Thank You that nobody will hurt him ever again.

A slap flew across her face, filling her head with pain and snapping her eyes open. Anna was out of her seat and in her face. Her eyes bulged. Her skin flushed with anger. "What did you do?"

Rage bubbled out of her lips in the same type of ugly tirade of insults and slurs as those that had kept Daisy and Fitz up so many nights. Her hand flew again. This time, Daisy blocked the blow and pushed her back. Anna fell to the floor, then she scrambled through the cabin to the cockpit.

The roar of the rising helicopter seemed to shake the air around Daisy. She looked down at Max and Fitz as they grew smaller and smaller below her, knowing there was no way she'd be able to jump from this height and survive. But Fitz and Max were together. She'd never imagined she'd meet anyone she cared about as much as Fitz. Let alone a man who'd care for Fitz the same way she did.

I don't want to leave either of them and I don't know how long Anna will keep me alive or what will happen next. But if I never see Max or Fitz again, protect them, Lord. Keep them safe. Fill their lives with happiness and love.

The helicopter shuddered beneath her, then

dropped so suddenly she felt her stomach lurch. The helicopter was descending and fast. Daisy grabbed Anna's headphones off the floor and slid them over her ears to hear what was happening in the cockpit.

"We have to go back!" Anna was shouting to Smith. "We need that baby! We have nothing without it!"

"Forget it!" Smith snapped. "They got Jones, Bradley and Kelly. We get out of here now and find another way to make the money without the baby!"

"There is no way without the baby!" Anna swore. "Gerry made sure there wouldn't be! Drop us back. I'll grab the baby and then we'll go."

The helicopter continued to drop, taking Daisy's stomach with it.

Twenty feet.

"I don't like it!" Smith shouted, his voice booming in the headphones.

Fifteen feet.

"You give me fire cover," Anna shouted. "I'll do it."

"You said no bullets and no shooting around the baby!"

Ten feet.

"I want the baby alive!" Anna snapped.

"Obviously! But I'd rather take him dead than not at all."

Eight feet.

The stairwell door flew open. Trent and Chloe burst through. Daisy watched as Max pushed baby Fitz into Chloe's arms and brushed a kiss across his head.

Then Max ran across the roof toward the helicopter as it lurched and dropped back down toward him.

Six feet.

Max leaped, grabbing the edge of the helicopter doorway with both hands, and climbed into the back of the air ambulance. It lurched up again, like Anna and Smith were battling for the controls, nearly tossing him back out again before he wedged his foot against the door.

Daisy yanked off the headphones and reached for him. His hand grabbed hers, and she pulled him into the helicopter. He dropped into the seat beside her.

"Anna and Smith are in the cockpit." She leaned toward his ear and shouted over the noise of the rotors. "I heard them in the headphones. Anna's trying to talk him into setting the copter down, so she can grab Fitz. She's telling Smith to open fire. To kill Fitz. To kill everyone, if that's what it takes."

"We won't let that happen!" he shouted. "Keep praying. Hold tight."

He brushed a kiss across her lips and made his way through the cabin. The cockpit door flew back and Anna stumbled out. Her eyes grew wide and she spun toward Max, holding the gun high, pointing it between his eyes.

The air ambulance swayed. Max leaped to the side, out of the range of fire, grabbed the gun with both hands and wrestled it from her grasp. The gun flew from her hand, rolling under the stretcher and tumbling through the boxes of equipment as it rolled and fell. Anna turned toward it, her eyes wild.

"Don't!" Max shouted.

But it was too late. Anna leaped for the weapon and she lost her footing. Terror filled her eyes as she slid back toward the open helicopter door. Daisy felt herself reach out to grab her boss and keep her from falling. "Anna! Please! Take my hand!"

Instead, a sneer turned on her boss's lips. She reached for the gun; the helicopter lurched, and as Daisy watched, Anna slipped and fell backward out of the helicopter with a scream and tumbled onto the rooftop below.

Her hands slid over her eyes. She couldn't watch Anna die, not again, no matter how evil she'd been and no matter how she'd taken advantage of the softness of Daisy's heart. Then she felt Max tumble into the seat beside her and grab her hand.

"It's okay. You can look. She's going to be okay." Max's voice was in her ear. She let him peel her hands off her face. She looked down and watched as Anna struggled to her feet, only to tumble back to the ground. A scream of rage flew from her lips and was swallowed up by the sound of the helicopter surging upward. They watched as Trent ran toward Anna, gun drawn.

"Broken leg, by the look of it," Max said. "She'll be fine. Trent will arrest her, doctors will patch her up and she'll sit in a jail cell in a cast, facing charges for kidnapping and attempted murder."

"Accomplice to Gerry's and Jane's murders," Daisy called into his ear, holding him tight. "Conspiracy, organized crime and forgery. She's the one who made the sugar maple money. She was behind the operation all the time, not Gerry."

Now Anna had been arrested. But Daisy and Max were still in the back of a helicopter as it accelerated rapidly. The hospital disappeared until it was nothing but a tiny box beneath them. Then the town faded and they were soaring over the Canadian wilderness.

Medical equipment tumbled out of the open back of the helicopter. Then boxes spilled open, tossing Fitz's baby toys, stuffed animals and model vehicles out into the forest below. It looked like they'd raided Fitz's nursery for every gift Gerry had ever given him before blowing the house up. What had Smith and Anna been planning? What role did Fitz play in it? And more important, where was Smith taking them now?

"Grab my legs and don't let go!" Max shouted. "I'm going to try to close the back of the helicopter door."

He dropped to the floor and slid toward the open door. She grabbed onto his feet as he hung out of the open doorway. Trees and rocks blurred far beneath him. The helicopter spun sharply, threatening to pull him from her grasp. A prayer crossed her lips.

His fingertips grabbed the door and he yanked it closed. It slammed, tossing him back into the helicopter. He stumbled to his knees and locked the door. Relief filled her lungs.

She expected Max to sit down again. Instead

he braced both of his hands on the back of her seat. His face hovered inches over her. "Now, I don't know where Smith is taking us or what he plans to do with us when he gets there, but I don't intend to find out. So I'm going to go convince him very nicely to turn around and take us back to the hospital." A determined smile turned on his lips. "Stay here and hold on tight, okay?"

Even kidnapped and held hostage in the back of a runaway helicopter being piloted by a killer and a madman, Max was still trying to reassure her. She adored that about him. She adored everything about him, and she knew, no matter what happened next, there was nowhere else she'd rather be.

She leaned forward and kissed him. He kissed her back. Then he pulled away from her, crawled through the cabin toward the cockpit.

Smith turned around and fired. The bullet flew past them and shattered the window. Air rushed through. Max grabbed Smith's arm and slammed it against the open doorway, breaking Smith's grasp on the gun. The helicopter spun, throwing Max into the cabin again. He struggled forward.

Smith reached under the seat and grabbed

something, and for a moment, she thought it was a second gun.

Then as she watched in horror, Smith threw on a parachute, yanked the door open and flung himself out of the helicopter. He disappeared beneath them.

They'd lost their pilot.

FIFTEEN

The air ambulance spun in free fall. Max flung himself into the pilot's seat. Wind beat at him through the open cockpit door. He yanked it closed and grabbed the seat belt to keep himself from falling through after Smith. Desperately, his hands and feet battled the controls, trying to keep them in the air. But it was too late. Smith had sabotaged the stabilization systems. They were going to crash. *Help me, God. What do I do?* He'd taken his pilot classes for fun. But he'd never tested. He'd never thought he needed to. Now, as he plummeted toward the ground, it was his only hope to keep Daisy alive.

He put the helicopter in autorotation, slowing the descent as his eyes searched the wilderness below, looking for a safe place to land. Treetops rose high around them. Jagged rocks shot out of the thick Ontario woods on all sides.

Then he saw it, a tiny sliver of gray blue shimmering in between the trees. A lake. He steered toward it. Behind him, he could hear things falling, crashing as they tumbled and tossed, and the sound of Daisy shouting prayers like a warrior's cry.

The ground rushed toward them. Thick rock filled his eyes. They weren't going to make it. He yanked the controls up and prayed, as he felt the updraft catch and toss them upward for a moment. Then a crash sounded around them. Everything shook like they'd just slammed into the ground and then unexpectedly fell through it.

Max's head snapped back against the seat. Pain filled his skull. Then he heard the sound of water roaring around the small metal copter like a thousand waves crashing around them.

Water flew past him on all sides and the helicopter sank into the lake. Cold seeped into his limbs, like something freezing and heavy was swallowing his body whole from the bottom up, threatening to drag him into unconsciousness.

Please, God. Don't let me die here today. I need to rescue her. I promised I'd protect her.

He gasped a breath, plunged underwater and yanked the cabin door open. Water filled the cabin. Equipment floated loose around him. He pushed through and swam down as his eyes searched the water for Daisy. Then he saw her. She was still strapped in the chair. Her eyes closed. Her blond hair floated loose around her. *No, please, no.*

Prayers filled his desperate heart as he swam for her. His hands struggled with the seat belt as his lungs fought for breath. Then she fell free.

He pulled her limp body into his arms and swam back for the cockpit. His mouth rose to the last few inches of air left in the cockpit and he gasped a final desperate breath. Then he pushed through the door and swam for the surface, pulling Daisy with him and battling the drag of the sinking helicopter as it threatened to pull Daisy from his arms. He didn't let go.

He surfaced in a lake, swam to shore and pulled Daisy up alongside him, cradling her limp body in his arms. He eased the water from her lungs, then slid his fingers along her throat and felt for her pulse.

"Keep fighting, Daisy! Please! I need you to fight!" He glanced back at the helicopter, watching the lifesaving equipment he needed sink deep below the surface. *Help me, Lord. Help me save her! Our story can't end now. It can't end like this.* Sirens sounded in the distance, far beyond the trees. "You hear that, Daisy? Police and paramedics are coming. They'll be here in a moment with oxygen. You just need to hold on for me, you can't die. Okay?"

Her pulse weakened against his touch. Then he felt it stop. He laid her back on the muddy ground and breathed deep into her lungs.

"You can't be dead, you hear me?" Tears filled his eyes as his hands pumped her core. "You're not allowed to leave me. Not now. Not like this. I need you to come back to me. Please, Daisy. I don't want to live without you."

Her eyelids fluttered. She coughed hard, spitting up water and then she looked up into his eyes. "Max?"

"Hey, Daisy." He pulled her into his chest. She reached for him, clutching him to her as if she was as frightened of losing him as he'd been of losing her. "Please don't ever leave me again. I don't ever want to lose you again."

"I won't." Her head fell against his chest. "I promise."

Beside them, the lake bubbled as the helicopter sank deeper. Fitz's baby toys and odd pieces of electronic equipment littered the ground around them. The sirens grew louder.

Then he saw figures running through the woods toward them, a virtual crowd of uniformed men and women—police, firefighters and emergency services—sweeping through the trees.

One tall figure ran forward and outpaced them all.

"Max!" Trent bellowed. "Come on, man! What did I tell you about flying a helicopter without a license?"

Deep laughter poured from Max's throat as he climbed to his feet and pulled Daisy up alongside him. "I'll get my license now. I promise! And it wasn't my fault, honest. The pilot decided to leave midflight."

"I know!" Amazement and affection filled Trent's gaze. "We saw him dangling from the trees a while back and sent some guys to pick him up. But it's still a mystery what he was doing, trying to fly off with boxes of baby gear stuffed with electronics."

Trent bent down, picked up a teddy bear and turned it over. Then he pulled the soggy fur apart and pulled out a small tablet. He pushed a button. "Password protected. Like everything else we've recovered since this whole thing started. I'm going to start praying for the tech guys. They're going to need all the help they can get cracking these."

"Well, he was pretty paranoid," Daisy said slowly, as if hearing herself say the words for the first time. Max watched as a thought began to form slowly behind her eyes. But whatever it had been faded as she saw Chloe striding through the crowd with a tiny form safe in her arms. "Fitz!"

Daisy ran toward Fitz. He reached for her and Max noticed for the first time the gentle-looking white-haired lady with nervous eyes standing a few feet behind them.

"Daisy, his aunt has come to take him," Chloe said. "We can't stay long. Her return flight leaves very soon. But I talked her into bringing him to say goodbye."

His heart lurched as he watched Daisy brush her fingers along the sides of Fitz's tender cheeks. Fitz waved his hands at her again and gurgled, his eyes growing wide when instead of pulling him into her arms, she took his tiny hand and let his fingers curl around hers.

"I'm sorry, Fitz," she whispered. "I'm afraid if I hold you now, I might never let you go. Now, you go be a good boy for your auntie. You grow brave and strong and know you're loved."

She brushed a kiss across his head and then

turned back as Chloe walked away with Fitz in her arms.

Lord, it wasn't fair! How could Daisy love someone so much and yet lose them? How could Max's own family have been torn apart by sorrow when he was only a couple of years older than Fitz?

Max's eyes scanned the ground covered with the toys, gadgets and electronics that represented a life that had been filled with money but not love. He'd never had anywhere near this many toys growing up. But he'd known he was loved and that had been what mattered.

He saw Daisy's eyes dim as they searched the ground, at the wreckage of a life she'd lived. She reached down and picked up a broken sailboat off the ground, and a sad sob left her lips.

"Gerry gave him this same boat the day he died," she said. "There was always a new present but it was never like there was any thought behind it. Then it was smashed to pieces in the crash."

She ran her fingers along the hull and then suddenly cracked it hard against her knee. It snapped in half. A bundle of sugar maple money and a small smartphone fell out. She turned the phone on. It was locked. The light in her eyes grew brighter.

"Chloe, wait!" Daisy called. She grabbed Max with one hand and they ran after her, Trent just one pace behind. Chloe stopped and Daisy slid the small device into Fitz's hand. He gurgled. His finger slid over the button.

The screen flashed. Fingerprint Password Accepted.

Trent whistled. "Hey, kid, try this one!" He slid the tablet he'd found in the teddy bear in front of Fitz. The baby scrunched his face at the device as his own reflection looked back at him. Then his eyes opened wide.

The device beeped and flashed the words *Retina Scan Accepted*. Data spilled onto the screen.

Trent shook his head. "I... Well... That's a new one..."

"Well, aren't you a little crime fighter?" Max chuckled softly. He slid his hand over Fitz's head. "I always knew you were a very special baby. It looks like you're going to get a whole bunch of devices to play with."

Then Max walked over to Fitz's aunt and stretched out a hand to shake hers. "I hope you know how amazing he is. If he ever needs anything, anything at all, you let me know."

He watched as Daisy gave Fitz a final kiss, then turned away and wrapped her arms around herself. Max ran after her, wrapped his arms around her and held her tightly. They stood there for a long moment, as they heard people come and go, processing the scene. Finally, Daisy's tears stopped, as if she'd cried her chest free of them. She tilted her face up toward him and her beautiful eyes met his.

"I need you to marry me, Daisy," he said. "I don't care if we have to date long-distance or if I have to figure out how to move to England or if you make me wait years and years for an answer. I can't lose you. Not like we lost Fitz and not like I thought I'd lost you earlier. You're the strongest, bravest, best part of me. And you make me a better man. Please be my wife."

She laughed, tears of happiness mingling with the tears of sadness on her cheeks. "Wait until you've known me longer than two days and then decide if you want to ask me again."

"Okay," he said. "But I already know that I will. I love you, Daisy."

"I love you, too, and I know what my answer will be," she whispered as he brought his lips to meet hers.

EPILOGUE

Deep, warm rays of August sunshine spread across the wooden farmhouse floor, casting her simple white beaded dress in hundreds of dazzling sparkles. Daisy pressed her hand against her chest. Her heart was so full of happiness, she thought it was going to explode.

A gentle knock sounded on the door.

"One moment!" Daisy took one last look at herself in the mirror. Her blond hair was curled in a braid and ringed in a crown of wildflowers. The vintage summer wedding dress she'd found in a secondhand store fell full and flowing down to her bare knees. She slid her feet into sandals.

Then she allowed herself one last glance outside the window. Six rows of folding chairs lay in two columns on the Henry farmhouse lawn, decorated with simple flowers she and Max's mother had picked.

Had it really only been a month since she'd finally accepted Max's proposal and five since Max had swept into her life and turned everything upside down? Eloping—that's what her aunt had called her whirlwind courtship when she'd called to invite them all to the wedding, despite the fact it didn't really count as an elopement when there was a ceremony.

But Daisy preferred to think of it as running. Running into the life she'd always wanted and never let herself dream she could ever find. Running into the arms of the incredible, remarkable man who loved her and whom she would love forever.

A man who'd somehow stretched his persuasive charm to the limits to convince Daisy's family to come to the wedding and used his own money to pay for their tickets. They'd all come, including Daisy's mother, aunt and all four of her half siblings, who now sat in the second row.

She watched as her stepfather squirmed under Max's brothers' watchful gazes. Apparently they'd given him a stern talking to—that at any flicker of anger or whiff of alcohol, they'd have him in handcuffs in seconds flat. He claimed he'd quit drinking and gambling and would never lay a hand on anyone ever again, and Daisy had no doubt the Henry brothers would sort out soon whether his contrition was true.

A second knock at the door. More rhythmic this time, like someone was playing percussion.

"One second!" She took one more glance out the window, hoping to catch a fleeting glimpse of her groom in the new blue jeans and crisp white shirt he and his brothers were wearing to the wedding. A sigh left her lungs. No Max. She scooped her bouquet of fresh field flowers off the bed and reached for the door. The handle turned.

A chuckle slipped through the doorway, cheerful and cheeky. Her heart stopped, her hands shook on the doorknob, as she pulled the door open. It couldn't be.

"Fitz!" Tears poured from her eyes, smudging her wedding makeup and sending it flowing down her cheeks as he stretched his pudgy hands out toward her.

"Dai!" He squealed, waving his arms. "Dai! Dai!"

A sob choked in her throat, the flowers fell to the floor as her arms wrapped around him and clutched him to her chest. Only then did she look up into the handsome, smiling face of the man who'd brought her precious baby back to her.

"Sorry to spring this on you," Max said softly. Emotion deepened his voice. He ran the back of his hand over his eyes. "But I only heard a couple of hours ago that his aunt was hoping to bring him, and I didn't want to get your hopes up until I had him in my arms and the papers in my hand."

She looked up over Fitz's head. "What papers?"

"Adoption." The single word choked with a sob in his throat. "Open adoption, actually. She felt so strongly ever since she saw us together that day in the woods that Fitz belonged with us. She told me to tell you she needed a few months to consult with a lawyer and her pastor. Then she called this morning to say she was in Ontario, meeting with the police—they found even more devices that Gerry had hidden—and asked if she could see us once they were done. So I invited her to the wedding."

"Our wedding!" Daisy blinked. She turned back to the mirror in shock, suddenly remembering where she was. Her carefully applied eye makeup now ran in sparkling gold and black streaks down her face. Fitz had yanked the crown of wildflowers from her hair and it now fell tattered and sideways. "I look a mess!"

"You look beautiful." Max stepped forward into the frame. His hand slid around her waist. "See, this is why I decided to risk interrupting you before the ceremony. I didn't want you to be walking down the aisle only to have Fitz yell for you, you to run to him and you both to delay the ceremony."

She laughed and leaned back into his chest. Her eyes ran over the three of them in the mirror, Fitz's cheeky grin beaming like that of the kind, warmhearted man who'd make such an excellent daddy. "I don't think I can let him go."

"That's okay." He turned her toward him, pulling Fitz into the safe crook between their chests. "You can hold him all the way through the ceremony and reception. As long as I can still slide a ring onto your finger and make you my wife."

"Deal." She leaned forward and kissed Max, hearing Fitz's giggle fill her ears and warm her heart as he held on to both of his new parents tightly.

* * * * *

If you enjoyed
THE LITTLEST TARGET,
look for these other books
by Maggie K. Black:

PROTECTIVE MEASURES
UNDERCOVER HOLIDAY FIANCÉE

Dear Reader,

Thank you for joining me for my second book about the Henry brothers. When I finished writing *Undercover Holiday Fiancée*, I worried I'd never discover another couple I liked as much as Trent and Chloe. But Max, Daisy and little Fitz really worked their way into my heart.

Right now, I'm writing this by the window in my favorite coffee shop. Usually I work from home with my two little dogs. But about once a week, I like to write here to get a different view of the world. Often I'm surrounded by business meetings. Occasionally, I witness either sweet or disastrous first dates. But this coffee shop also gets a steady stream of people in uniform, especially paramedics. It's not unusual for me to pop my head up and ask them random questions like, "Who gets to fly the helicopter?" or "What tools do you have on your belt?" I'm extremely thankful for their patience! All creative mistakes in this book are my doing, not theirs.

Thank you again to all the amazing readers who've got in touch with your thoughts, questions and suggestions. I really enjoy hearing from you! I'm sorry I've got behind in responding to physical letters, but I'll take a trip to the post office as soon as this book is done. You can find me on Twitter at @MaggieK-Black or at www.maggiekblack.com.

Thank you all for sharing this journey with me,
Maggie

Get 2 Free Books,
Plus 2 Free Gifts—
just for trying the Reader Service!

Get 2 Free Books,
Plus 2 Free Gifts—
just for trying the
Reader Service!

HARLEQUIN
HEARTWARMING™

HOME *on the* RANCH